The
Great
Shock

Evajean Blum Blackstone

ISBN: 9798488971646

Imprint: Independently published

Dedication
To Marj Hinds
My friend.
My editor.
My best critic.
My deepest thanks for being tough and honest!
Never could have done this without you!

Medical Acknowledgements:
Jon Keeve, MD, Orthopaedic Surgeon
John Shuster, MD, Orthopaedic Surgeon

Surgical treatment of arterial lower-limb injuries by fire arms

Bilel Derbel, Jalel Ziadi, Sobhi Mleyhi[*]**, Rim Miri, Malek Ben Mrad, Faker Ghédira, Raouf Denguir**
Department of Cardiovascular surgery, la Rabta Hospital,Medical institute of Tunis. Tunis EL MANAR University, Tunisia

Corresponding Author:
    Sobhi Mleyhi
    Department of Cardiovascular surgery
    la Rabta Hospital, Medical institute of Tunis
    Tunis EL MANAR University, Tunisia

4

Acknowledgements:
Adrienne Richardson
Thank you, my dear friend, my temporary roommate, my confidant, for those many mornings in our jammies endlessly discussing scenarios over coffee, and for your great longsuffering as you were coerced into reading every page as it came off the printer.

Bruce and Alisa Cardin
Mike and Donna Hrehor
Thank, you my dear friends, for reading the book in its infancy and for your great suggestions and your loving encouragement.

My daughters.
Holly & Chelsea
Thank you for pushing me to do this!

Cover Art
Thank you to Bailey Deale, my 12-year-old 7th grader cousin from Portland Oregon. She loves all things visual arts and says that drawing original compositions makes her happy and gives her a sense of accomplishment to see her original vision come to life.

Chapter 1

It was one of THOSE days. This time it was a Wednesday. Not that there hadn't been other Wednesdays. But this was the latest one. Elle sat on the floor where she had landed with a thud after Butch had slammed her there with his fist in her chest. His last words reverberated in her head.

"You are a---" She couldn't even say the words out loud. It was horrifying that they were screaming inside her head. Tears flowing, she bowed her head wondering for the hundredth time why she had ended up like this. Where had she gone wrong? How could she have been so stupid?

After a while she looked up realizing she must have dozed off. It was dark everywhere. The house was dark. Pitch black outside. She pulled herself to a standing position and stretched out her cramped muscles. In the bathroom, she stared at herself in the mirror. A fine white dust covered her hair and face. It looked like she had been too close to a wild pastry chef. But no. She knew without looking at the wall just barely above where she had been standing, there would be a hole the size of Butch's fist. She shook her head, ruffling her hair. It rained sheet rock dust. She splashed water on her face and looked at her reflection.

"Yeesh," she said, "I look like I was dumped out of a vacuum cleaner!" Two rivulets of black mascara trickled down through the chalky paste, dropped off her chin landing on her shirt. "At least it wasn't as bad as last time." She grimaced, thinking about the split lip, and black eye. "Well?" she said to the reflection. "Are you going to stand here feeling sorry for yourself? When are you going to finally change your ways? Is this the last straw? Have you been humiliated enough?" She stared at the face looking back at her and nodded. "Yup. This is the end of the road, Butchie Boy. I'm quitting while I still have a shred of self-respect. Going to the kitchen right now to have a drink to celebrate my decision," she answered herself out loud. After washing her face again, dusting off the rest of her clothes she headed to the kitchen.

Fridge door open, she stared unseeingly at the various liquid beverages while those last words of Butch's slashed through her mind. "Oh, for some kind of quick amnesia about now," she said to the tequila. Not wanting to dull her mind, she ignored Butch's tequila, choosing club soda instead. Then she spied a diet Pepsi, more to her liking, removed it and slammed the fridge door, cringing at the sound of resulting dangerous clanking from inside.

Standing in the middle of the kitchen, she opened the soda and guzzled about a third of the bottle. Her eyes watered. Her throat burned. Then she felt a giant, very unladylike belch rising to the surface. Soda in one hand, cap in the other, no time to try to contain it, out it came, very loud.

"There it is. The final punctuation to six terrible years. Well, mostly terrible." She sighed. "Six years." She shook her head. "That's... let's see... twenty-six divided by six is four with two left over. That's a quarter of my life that I will never see again. Pretty sad commentary for a nice girl from the suburbs. Tomorrow I change the locks, then pack up all his stuff to gift it to Goodwill, or the dumpster." She smiled, enjoying the idea of the dumpster.

Soda still in hand, she stood in the doorway of the bedroom she had shared with him for six years. Why? Why did she let him stay so long? She should have tossed him out after the first time he put his hands around her neck, or at least when he gambled away her whole paycheck. She felt so stupid. The whole reason she didn't marry him was because she wasn't sure about him. It wasn't long until she realized he was a textbook manic depressive, or bipolar, or whatever they call it these days, narcissist. Yet, she let him stay.

What was wrong with her brain? The worst of it was that she had been brought up better than this.

She put the lid back on her soda and threw the bottle on the bed. Then she sighed loudly. The tears began to trickle. She slapped them away, turned with a vengeance and marched back down the hall to the kitchen for trash bags. Back in the bedroom, she yanked open drawers, pulled things out, and stuffed it all into the trash bags. Then she started on the closet. Then the floor. All the time, muttering to herself. He was such a slob! Empty cigarette packs, half eaten sandwiches, empty chip bags, empty whisky bottles and candle wax everywhere. Toys! Yes, TOYS! Stupid man. He was a child in a man's body! Including the tantrums! "Take me to the store right now! I can't discuss anything with you. I'm out of cigarettes!" Big baby. Could not keep a dime in his pocket! Was always broke. Blew every cent of his money and hers on candles, booze, and toys. She maxed out her credit cards buying him clothing and necessities so he could spend his money on junk! Gahhh! Could she be any stupider? Was that a real word? More stupid? She glanced at the clock, 2:00 a.m. She wasn't tired. She was too angry.

Down on the floor on her hands and knees on his side of the bed she picked up candy wrappers, dirty dishes, magazines, stubs of burned candles, and more of the same in the nightstand. "Oh, yay, his check book." Balance? Who knows? He never paid any attention. He used his debit card until it was declined. She was sure he'd never heard of a check register. Or, God forbid, reconciliation of a bank statement. She grimaced. Her mother, who would search for a penny if she didn't balance, would have a stroke if she knew how Butch handled money. She felt a sneeze coming on. "A-a-CHOO!" She seriously needed to clean house or hire someone to do it. But maybe not until after the slob was gone for good. Her back was beginning to hurt, so she sat up and leaned against the wall. Drawers in the nightstand were empty. Dare she look under the bed? She lifted the edge of the comforter with her bare foot. She cringed, thinking something might pop out and bite her. Not surprised, she viewed the dust bunnies, more candy wrappers, a few coins, a comb, some underwear, a couple of books, another check book. "A-a-CHOO!" Wow! Two sneezes! That was something! Her friend, Anna, could sneeze ten times in a row. Elle could sneeze once and that was usually it. She loved to sneeze. She even wrote a term paper about sneezing when she was in school. She envied Anna. Wait. What was this? Too big to be a check book. Curious, she lay flat on the floor so she could get her head almost under the bed. The man was a slob. She reached in and pulled it closer. Not a check book. A book. A black book. She scowled. Yup, that's what she's always wanted to see. Her boyfriend's black book. Gee, only one? Well? Might as well learn something.

She sat back against the wall again, trash bag on her lap, and flipped pages. It was his usual scraggly handwriting. As she read, her eyes widened, and her heartbeat soared to warp speed. This was no ordinary black book! This was weird. Her head felt like it might spin around and fly off.

This wasn't right. She shook her head. This belonged to someone else. This wasn't the Butch she knew. She took a deep breath. If this was Butch's book, what was this? For a job? Had he gone into some kind of business? Doing what?

She flipped through the rest of the pages. She didn't understand a lot of it, but she knew it wasn't good. This was devastation. This was … What was it? She felt sick. She couldn't think. Suddenly she was cold. Her teeth began to chatter. She returned to her sitting position on the floor, then pulled the comforter off the bed and wrapped up in it. She sat there on the floor like a mummy beside the bed, leaned her head back and wondered what to do. She couldn't understand what had happened to Butch. There was a time when he was sweet and loving and thoughtful! She shut her eyes and tried to think of something he did that was nice.

Chapter 2

She was awakened by the yellow rays of Thursday morning's sunshine warming her face. She opened her eyes and looked around. Why was she on the floor? Why was there no feeling in her legs? Oh. The trash bag. She attempted to stand up. Her body strenuously objected. Her head hurt. Her eyes felt like raw hamburger. She changed her mind and stayed on the floor.

She looked around for her phone, and something caught her eye. Turning her head, both eyes connected with something sticking out from between the mattress and box spring. Yanking off the comforter had revealed the unexpected. More candy wrappers? An empty twinkie packet? Porno magazine? No. Something green. She reached out and pulled on it. Out came a big wad of cash! Her mouth fell open. She gaped. Really? She reached in and pulled out more. And then more. And then more. "Holy Cow!" she croaked. She painfully pulled herself to a standing position and gave the mattress a push. More bills came to light. She lifted the mattress and looked around. When she was satisfied there was nothing else under there, she let the mattress down and stood up straight. "Oww!" She moved different parts of her body, attempting to un-kink. Improvement. Now she was wide awake.

She looked down at the pile of money on the floor and wondered where on earth it had come from. What was she going to do with it? Butch was a gambler, but this was a lot, even for him! He could have had a big win, but it was highly unlikely. Did he win the lottery? No. That's stupid. She had never known him to buy a ticket. Was it real? Did he rob a bank? Steal it from someone? What had Butch gotten himself into? She probably should count it. But first, coffee. Her head hurt. She needed coffee. A lot of coffee.

She headed down the hall and stopped off at the bathroom. She looked at herself in the mirror and wondered if there had been a time when she looked worse.

Futile attempts to freshen up completed, she stood in the kitchen in front of the Keurig. In moments, the fresh hot coffee was warming her throat. It felt good going down. "Nectar of the gods," she always said. Fingers curled around the handle of her cup, she ambled out through the kitchen door to the deck and chose a comfy chair near the house where the sun hadn't yet touched.

She stuck her feet out from the shade into the September sunshine and frowned at her bright red toenails. She needed a pedicure. She had smeared her right big toe when she was getting into the car after her last appointment, and it had annoyed her every time she noticed it.

Her love of red was further revealed in her yard, both front and back. Near her on the deck, were several large pots of Begonias, bright red against the white railing, warming their giant blossoms in the sun. Trees and flowers flourished beyond the deck railing as well. It was all designed with tranquility in mind. The front of her house continued in the same vein, a white story book front porch and picket fence. Red begonias cascaded over the porch railing, and of course, to complete the perfect picture, a red door.

Working out of town so much made it even more of a pleasure to come home, especially when Butch was off doing whatever he did when he'd disappear for days at a time. In the beginning, they would sit out on the deck in the evenings and visit until it got too chilly. But now, she reveled in her alone time. As Butch's behavior had disintegrated, she looked forward less and less to coming home. She'd go to Linda's or Mandy's and kill time.

She used to ask him where he had been. He'd always say it was none of her business. "Do I ask you where you've been?" Sarcasm was his tone of choice lately. She'd think, "You know where I am – working!"

With a great sigh, she stood up and returned to the kitchen. She set her coffee cup on the counter and dialed a number. "George, oh good, you're up. Oh, you're not? Oh, so sorry. But now that you're awake, I need to see you this morning. It's really important. I mean really important. Ok. Thank you. See you at ten."

She cried a bit in the shower, but she was determined not to give Butchie Boy the benefit of any more tears. She stepped out of the shower and wrapped her hair in a towel and her body in another one. She eyed herself in the mirror. Water droplets from stray blond curls, escapees from the towel on her head, glistened on her cheek. Big blue eyes stared back. She licked her lips, puckered up, and then stuck her tongue out. That made her feel better. She padded down the hall to her room, donned her fluffy robe, and sat down at the dressing table to do her face.

That done, she took the towel off her head and used various bottles and tubes from her vast supply of products designed to un-frizz or prevent frizz or touch up frizz. It was a never-ending frizzy struggle. Scrunching her hair, dryer on low, attempting to prevent frizz, she gave her head a shake and looked for something to wear. She chose a pair of black jeans, added a red knit top and black jeweled flip flops, grabbed her red lipstick and her black sequined bag and was out the door by 9:30.

Once she was on the road, she decided she needed breakfast. She made a few turns and ended up in McDonald's Drive Thru. When it was her turn to order she told her conscience to shut up and chose her usual: two sausage cheese biscuits and a caramel frappe. She ate the two biscuits on the way to George's office, pulled into the parking garage, wound her way up to Level Twelve and found a spot to park. After one last gulp of the frappé, she pulled down the visor and checked the mirror and reapplied lipstick. Finishing the frappé would have to wait. It was sticky on the outside of the cup anyway. She reached in the glove box for a baby wipe and rid her hands of the stickiness. Then she got out of the car and stood outside to brush off any remaining crumbs. She checked her face in the side mirror and locked the car.

She walked the short distance to the railing and stood for a moment admiring the view of the city from George's building. It wasn't the tallest building in Portland, but if office buildings could be called pretty, she'd definitely say the Stanford Building in beautiful downtown Portland, Oregon had all the virtues necessary. First of all, it was majestic in white brick and glass. Secondly, it rested on the banks of the Willamette River, a most spectacular view from any floor. The offices on one side of the building looked out over the city with the mountains in the background. On a clear day one could see Mount Hood. The offices on the other side overlooked the river.

She gave a great sigh and turned to the task at hand. At the private door, she tapped the numbers on the keypad and let herself in. She wandered through the dark hallways out to the spacious front lobby where she met George. He walked her into his office and held the door for her. She flopped into one of the overstuffed chairs while he went around and sat across from her at his desk.

"Is this an attorney thing or a friend thing?" He smiled at her trying to get her to smile back. She didn't smile. She just pulled the black book out of her purse and handed it to him. He leaned back in his chair and opened it. His eyes widened. His chair hit the wall and bounced him forward against his desk.

"Where on God's green earth did you get this?"

"Under the bed," she said dryly. "Where else?"

"Do you know how long it's been under there?"

Elle rolled her eyes. "Uh... my cleaning lady has fallen ill."

George snickered. "Did she fall or is she ill?"

Elle rolled her eyes again. "Very funny. I've been gone a lot."

George leaned forward. "You know, don't you, that one of these days your eyeballs won't come all the way around. They'll be stuck in the back of your head." He thought a minute. "Which might not be a bad thing! Won't that be handy if you ever have kids?"

Elle nearly rolled her eyes again but caught herself. "You were asking how long this thing has been under the bed?" She sighed. "No idea… days…? weeks…? months…?"

He leaned closer to her. "Do you know what you have here?"

"No. I mean, I'm not sure. Sort of. No. Not really. It just looks bad."

"It IS bad!" he squeaked in falsetto.

"Shhhh! Do you want Linda to hear you??"

"Sorry. Lost my head. You know, don't you, that I shouldn't see this? I'm an officer of the court! I can't know this stuff!" His voice began to crescendo.

She waved her arms at him. "Shhhhh!," she whispered tersely. "Can you at least get me another restraining order?"

"Again? Again. Jeez. Yes. Let's do that right now." He dug around in his drawer for the paperwork. "And you cannot tell a living soul about this!"

She rolled her eyes. "Who would I tell??? Are you serious?" She sighed. "Oh, George, I'm so sorry. I sound mad. Well, I am, but not at you, ok?"

George grinned. "It's ok. I can handle it. I'm tough."

Elle grinned back. "I can still take you."

George grinned. "Uh. We were seven and you weighed more than me, fluffy. I work out now. Check out these guns!" He flexed for her. "Hey, do you want to run Bloomsday with me next Spring? We'll go to Spokane for the weekend and see friends and do the run on Sunday morning!"

Elle rolled her eyes again. She really needed to stop that. She was beginning to get another headache. "No. Running with 150,000 sweaty bodies in really cool running gear and being followed by thousands of wheelchairs and strollers is not my idea of fun." She grinned. "You know me. I hate to sweat. Now, back to our regularly scheduled program? There's more." She handed him a big manila envelope. When he looked inside, he seemed a bit pale.

"Where did THIS come from?"

"Between the mattress and the box springs on HIS side of the bed."

"Did you count it?"

"Twenty thousand dollars."

He gently laid the envelope down on his desk. They both stared at it.

The phone rang and they both jumped.

Chapter 3

The telephone kept ringing. Elle looked across the desk at George, who had apparently gone deaf. He seemed mesmerized by that envelope. The phone continued to ring.

There was a loud knock on the door. They both jumped again like spooked cats. George's sister, Linda, also his Legal Assistant, appeared in the crack of the doorway. George finally tore his eyes away from the envelope and looked up.

"It's Judge Nickerson's office. She says it's urgent."

"Ok, thanks, Sis." He squeezed the bridge of his nose, shut his eyes for a moment in an effort to return to the current reality, and lifted the receiver.

Trying not to eavesdrop, Elle studied her toenail polish while she waited, and was reminded once again of the necessity to make an appointment for a pedicure. She frowned again and decided to ignore her feet for now. Then she decided to mentally add it to her To Do list, chuckling, knowing full well that mental lists were immediately AWOL and it was futile to say, "I'll make a mental note." She pulled out her phone and added the reminder to her real To Do list on her Notes app, acknowledging that even putting it on the Notes app wasn't a guarantee she'd remember, since it required her to actually check the Notes app occasionally.

She watched George talk on the phone. His unruly red hair, still damp from the shower, probably after running his customary five miles this morning, seemed to be quite calm. His eyes were sky blue, which Elle had always believed made him look trustworthy. His pale skin was clear except for a sprinkling of freckles, not so many that if they grew together, they could be a tan.

He had turned out to be a really great human, and in spite of the fact that he was a genius, he was nice. He was nice to everyone. He never lorded his intelligence over people. He treated everyone with respect, regardless of age, looks, color, political opinions, etc. She had always been very proud of him for his integrity and his work ethic.

He had followed his father into the law, not because his father demanded it, but because he strongly believed that he could make a difference. So, in spite of his academic prowess, this summa cum laude graduate of Gonzaga Law School cared about people who couldn't afford a lawyer. She loved him for that--like a brother. To his credit, he was already on retainer from some high-powered clients, which in itself was remarkable since he was fresh out of law school. His reputation for honesty and competence had already drawn the attention of several large companies headquartered in Portland. Thankfully these clients seemed to be able to comfortably support him with their generous retainers, thereby enabling him to take on pro bono clients, or what she called his flock of ugly ducklings.

She yawned, stood up and stretched and wandered out to say hi to Linda.

Linda smiled. "How are you, Honey?"

"I've been better, but I made a decision last night. I'm finally permanently extricating myself from Butch. I'm so done with him! We had a slight altercation. No. Butch had an altercation and I got in the way. But that just spurred me to finally do the right thing."

Linda grinned. "Oh, I'm so glad! Now, can you finally marry my brother?"

Elle grinned. "He certainly doesn't hide his feelings!"

Linda smiled too. "Our dads sure would be pleased, wouldn't they?"

Elle nodded. "My dad would be relieved! Your dad would be happy! My dad has suffered for six years with Butch, and I know he wishes I'd move on. Both Mom and Dad have tried so hard to be nice and he just blows them off. He'll go to family dinners with me and he'll just jump up from the table and disappear. He has no manners. Never asks to be excused. Never tells my mom thanks for dinner. I swear some days he's schizophrenic! He can be so charming and the next minute so rude and insensitive! Well, YOU know how it is! You've been there sometimes when we're all together. You've seen it with your own eyes."

"I'm sorry, Sweetie. I know it's been hard. We put up with him because we love you. If you really are finished with him, it would make things so much more fun on our family winter ski trips and summers at the lake. Butch made everything so awkward." Linda put her hand over her mouth. "Oh. Sorry. That wasn't very nice."

Elle sighed. "But it's true and we all know it. By the way, have you talked to Mandy? Are we doing something this weekend while our dads are hunting? And by the way, why are you here?"

Linda smiled. "Well, I get to see you!"

Elle rolled her eyes. "Very funny. I'm so flattered! No, really, you're supposed to have the week off. Don't the dads give everyone the week off when they go hunting?"

Linda pointed to the stack on her desk. "I wanted to reduce this pile if I can, and since George was coming in to meet you, I thought I might as well do it now. So, are you in for shopping and lunch this weekend? Thirsty Lion? Yes, Mandy's in. Oh, when do you fly again?"

"Ohhhh… how you tempt me!" Elle looked at the calendar on her phone. "Yes! I wanna! I work on Monday. I fly to Dallas in the morning. I deadhead. You know? I fly from Portland to Dallas to catch my flight to Sydney. Did I ever explain deadheading?"

Linda smiled affectionately. "Yes, I think you have mentioned it. Are you sick of flying yet?" She knew how much Elle loved her job.

Elle beamed rapturously. "It's still a thrill every time we take off and I adore Australia!" As a flight attendant, right now, her assignment was Dallas to Sydney. She had dreamed of being a flight attendant ever since she could remember. She had never wanted to do anything else.   And now she was living her dream, but this past year she had requested that particular route because it gave her a chance to spend more hours away from Butch.

Elle heard George saying good-bye. "I swear, Lin, you talk to my sister more than I do! Let me know what time on Saturday."

Linda winked at her and said, "OK! G'day!"

Elle laughed out loud and waved as she disappeared into George's office.

George hung up and sighed. "They've moved a court date for one of my clients, so I need to be ready to go tomorrow morning at ten. And guess what? They can't find the idiot. They've put out an APB. Could I ever just have an intelligent client for once??"

"Hmph! Does that include me??"

"Oh, Elle, of course not. You don't count. I mean, you are in a class all by yourself!"

"Well, if you would stop taking all these pro bonos. What do you expect when you defend the flotsam and jetsam of humanity?"

"Sure," he said, "I'll just take a moment and give each client the Wechsler. Will that be satisfactory?"

"Perfect!" Elle smiled wickedly. "But I'm wondering just how many of your clients could actually finish the test -- let alone pass it."

"How about I just advertise in the Mensa Newsletter?"

"Uh do they have one?" Elle looked at her phone. "I'll just google it and see. Well! Would you believe? They do! It's a magazine called the Mensa Bulletin! I wonder if you can subscribe if you're not a member... Hmmm... "

"Elle, I was just kidding. I like what I do, in spite of the prevailing insanity and lunacy. In the meantime, could we talk about this envelope?"

"No. Let's not. Gahh! Why don't you stick that thing in your safe so I don't have to look at it?"

He stood up and turned to go to the safe. Then he paused and looked at Elle. "Turn your back. You can't see this." He headed towards the door behind his desk and entered his private suite.

"Oh, George, I don't care about the combination to your safe. Don't be ridiculous. Ok. Fine. See? Turning my back. Why don't you just shut the door so I can't see? " She stood up and turned to face the other way.

George's dad and Elle's dad, best friends since boyhood in Spokane, both had wanted to study law and were accepted to Gonzaga Law School. In their usual fashion of doing so many of the same things, they had met their wives at Gonzaga and had each been the best man at their respective weddings the summer before graduation.

They had kicked around the idea of moving to the Oregon coast and, like all good husbands, after discussing it with their wives, they decided together to make the move. They packed up, migrated west, and set up the firm of Wendling & Wickersham on the twelfth floor of a beautiful building downtown Portland, Oregon. The view from their offices was spectacular: the great Columbia River, the Willamette River watershed, and Mt. Hood. So, they didn't make it all the way to the coast. But now it was only an hour and half to the beach.

The whole twelfth floor was divided into four corner suites. When the elevator arrived, the first step was immediately into the lobby. The right front quadrant was the spacious main reception area. Two receptionists greeted clients and answered phones. Behind was the staff lounge with full kitchen, restrooms, comfortable chairs and couches, a Keurig with its partner carousel and gleaming espresso machine. Next to the kitchen was the conference room. A large window in the kitchen opened into the conference room for passage of food and beverages. Next to the conference room was a smaller office containing transcription and records. Then beyond was a large office shared by two interns. The back two quadrants were the partners' offices, Jim Wickersham on the right and Bob Wendling on the left.   In the center, for waiting clients, there were comfortable groupings of chairs arranged among greenery and warmed by sunshine from the skylight. Also in the center was a Keurig with a large carousel filled with k-cup pods in a variety of flavors.

The front left quadrant was a duplicate of the other two. That was George's office. The three offices each contained a private suite with a small bath, a kitchenette and a pleasant living area with several comfortable couches, and a big screen TV. Just inside the door of each of the suites were what looked like ancient steam heaters. They were actually the safes.

Elle could hear the buzzing noises of the dial going back and forth and then the clang of the door opening. And then, the door slamming shut and the dial spinning. George came back into the office closing the door behind him.

Suddenly there was a commotion in the outer office and a scream. George sprinted to the door and listened for a moment before flinging the door wide open. Elle stood in the middle of the room frozen.

Two men were standing center stage with guns pointed at George.

Chapter 4

George put his hands up and yelled, "Linda! Where are you? Are you ok?"

A tiny voice came from somewhere beyond his vision. "I'm here under my desk and I'm f-fine!" Her voice was wobbly, but she was alive.

George breathed a sigh of relief and stretched all the way up to his six-foot four-inch height, but he kept his hands up. "What is going on out here?" he boomed with a confidence he did not feel. "Why is my secretary under her desk?"

The men were both wearing black Fedoras, expensive charcoal gray Brioni suits and black Gucci loafers. Elle stifled a nervous laugh. She wanted to say, "Who are you guys supposed to be? Did I miss Halloween?" She wondered if Elliot Ness was out in the corridor. Was there a 1929 Chrysler waiting at the curb?

The short guy had a fat cigar in his mouth. He told George, around the cigar that seemed fastened to his lower lip, to stay there and not come any closer.

George kept his hands up but tried some diplomacy. "We are happy to help you. There is no need for guns. Just tell me what you need and I'll try to accommodate. I'd even feel more helpful if you didn't point the gun at us."

"Relax. Your secretary scuttled under there like a scared chicken! And well she should, cuz I ain't the best of shots!" He guffawed at his joke. He wiggled his gun and then pointed it at Elle. "You must be Elle. Butch said you was pretty, but he didn't really tell the truth! Yer a lot more prettier than he said. Yer a hottie! We thought we might find you here. And here you are!" He guffawed, apparently entertained by his wit. "Butch has always suspected there was something going on between you two. Heh. Heh. Heh. But right now, all we need is to find Butch. He keeps sneaking away. They kicked him outta Vegas and Reno so who knows where he goes to gamble now? You'll have to tell us where he is. So, be a nice pretty girl and tell us what we want to know." He waggled the gun again.

Elle's mouth was dry. Her lips were stuck together. As she watched cigar ashes float down to the carpet, she felt a trickle of sweat roll down the middle of her back. This was scary. This guy was seriously disturbed. He probably would shoot someone just for fun! The cold fingers of fear began to clutch her heart. She had never been shot at or taken a bullet and she wasn't about to start now. She took a few steps back, away from the door and tried to speak with calm assurance, but her words came out in gasps. "Why do you need to find him?"

George stepped in front of her. "Just wait a minute, Elle." He turned to the two men. "Just what are your intentions?"

Elle had already named them the Mutt and Jeff. They reminded her of a cartoon in the daily newspaper that her dad and grandfather liked. She had always thought it weird that Mutt was the tall one. She guessed it was all part of their charm. She had looked them up online and discovered that the artist Harry Fisher had started drawing them in 1907 and the cartoon had been syndicated across the United States. She was reminded about them when she discovered a movie from the 1970's called the Sting, which became one of her favorite movies of all time. In the 1973 film *The Sting,* Robert Redford's character Johnny Hooker refers to the mark's bodyguards as "Mutt and Jeff".

But these gangsters were not cartoons. Jeff, the shrimpy one that seemed oddly enough to be the boss, spoke again. "I told you to stay back. You're really not in a position to be the one asking questions, are you? It seems that I'm the one with the gun, just to clarify things. And by the way, you don't have much security around here do you? The office seems kinda empty. Did we scare them all away? Heh. Heh. Heh.." He was amused by his own humor.

George took a tiny step backward. "Of course. Please go ahead."

The front door burst open, and a voice screeched "Goooooood Morrrrrrnning!!"

There was a gun shot and George yelled, "Hit the deck!" Coffee and donuts flew everywhere, and bodies hit the floor.

Elle lay still, frightened, her eyes shut, her hands on her head, wondering if that gunman had been startled by Gus (poor Gus!) and accidentally pulled the trigger. She wondered if anyone was dead or injured and was relieved to hear Linda whimpering (she hoped it was Linda) and a loud "ouch" from Gus, which meant that at least those two were alive.

Wishing desperately to know if George was alive, she heard the sound of running feet and the door opening and slamming shut. She wondered if those were the gunmen running away. Then she wondered what kind of gangsters actually ran away. Maybe they'd decided things were going wrong and it would be just too messy to shoot them all. After all, they seemed to need information, so killing them all wouldn't be that helpful. Poor Gus. Poor unsuspecting Gus. Poor Gus -- that may have saved their lives!

Elle raised her head slightly and breathed a deep sigh of relief. George was alive and sitting up, looking at Gus. She decided then and there she'd stop getting after George for eating donuts every day, since he never seemed to gain an ounce anyway, no matter what he put in that bottomless pit. She crawled over towards George.

"George! Thank God, you're alive! And thank God we're all alive!"

George pointed across the office. "Linda's monitor is dead." They all looked and sure enough, there was a gaping bullet hole in the middle of her computer screen.

"Gus, are you ok?" George patted Elle's head and crawled over to where Gus was still face down on the carpet, surrounded by

George's standing order of two Maple Bars, two Blueberry scones, one Caramel Macchiato, one sugar free lemon poppy seed muffin and a skinny latté.

Gus groaned and looked up at George. "Are they really gone? This is going to cost you extra, George." He rolled over to reveal two smashed venti coffee cups stuck to his shirt surrounded by a very large coffee colored stain, through which one could just barely make out "Gus, the Pastry Guru" embroidered in red on his shirt pocket. There was a very flat maple bar stuck to his forehead.

Elle hurried over to Linda to help her up and see if she was ok. George managed to help Gus to his feet and arrange his ample body on the couch, losing all hope of saving it from coffee and doughnut fallout. He left to get some paper towels. When he came back, Gus was staring into space, overwhelmed by the events of the past few minutes. George removed the maple bar from Gus' head and tossed it with a sad farewell into the waste basket. He was starving. He wiped the gooey maple frosting from Gus' forehead with a wet paper towel and dried him off with a second dry one.

"Gus, can you navigate?"

Gus groaned again and got to his feet. "I'm going to need a stiff drink before I go."

"You can't drink! It's still morning! Isn't it?" Elle looked at her Fitbit. "Well, it's almost lunch time. I need to go home. Wait. I don't think I'm going home. Maybe I'll take a vacation. To Pluto. " She looked at George. "What are we going to do? Who do you think those men were?"

"Well, I doubt they were Jehovah's Witnesses." He grinned.

"Very funny." Elle frowned at him. "How can you make light of this situation? We came pretty close to death!"

"Hey, we're alive! That's a good thing!"

"I'm leaving," Gus announced. "I've got more orders to deliver and now I'm way behind!" He flapped his hand at them and as he stepped outside, he bellowed, "That smorgasbord on your carpet is going on your bill, George! AND laundry services!"

"Wait." George stopped him. "The police are going to want to get a statement from you."

"I didn't see anything! I have no statement to make except my clothes are all dirty and you, my friend, will be getting a laundry bill!"

George debated for thirty seconds and said, "They'll call you if they need your statement. Go ahead. Don't forget. We're out of the office the rest of the week."

Gus headed out and George waved his goodbye to the closing door and said, "Yah, yah, I know the last thing we all expected was a couple of hoodlums with guns."

Elle was helping Linda out from under her desk. "What are we going to do, George?"

"Well," George stood still, pinched the bridge of his nose and closed his eyes to collect his thoughts. "First of all, I'm very glad our dads are out of the office, hunting. And I'm even more thankful they always give everyone the week off, so it's just us they frightened. Now, we call the police." He opened his eyes, reached for his cell phone and dialed 911. He explained the circumstances and listened for instructions. "No. No one was hurt. Just one gun shot to one of our computer monitors. Yes. I understand. Thank you."

George looked at the girls. "They're sending someone to take statements from us and look over what happened." He looked at Elle. "I think we should check you into a hotel with a fake name, at least until we can figure out who those men are and what they want."

"You and I both know what they want." Elle frowned at George.

The three of them sat in Linda's office waiting for someone from the Portland Police Bureau.

George tapped his foot. "I don't think we should mention the black book just yet. That may open a huge can of worms."

Elle nodded. "I agree. Let's not go there."

Linda looked questioningly at George. "What am I not supposed to talk about?"

George said, "We'll tell you later but it's good right now you don't know anything about that."

Linda smiled hesitantly. "I guess I should be happy ignorance is bliss."

Elle smiled conspiratorially. "I agree!"

The authorities arrived in the shape of two uniformed police officers and a third person, Jack Benson, who turned out to be a forensic tech, and friend of George's, who immediately set up to do finger printing. He took the prints of all three of them so they would be able to identify as many prints as possible. They showed their badges and ID and identified themselves as Dennis Armstrong and James Lawson. Elle thought they were awfully young to be policemen, but if they went straight to academy after high school, it would seem possible. She felt old.

Officer Armstrong examined the injured computer monitor after Jack had dug the bullet out, looked around at the coffee and frosting stains on the floor, and got descriptions of the gunmen. The three witnesses took turns explaining to Officer Lawson the sequence of events. When all three had given a full account to the satisfaction of both officers and answered all the questions, the officers departed with the request that they all go down to the station and sign their statements as soon as possible. Jack was the last one out. He shook hands with George and suggested lunch some time. George told him that would be great.

"OK, girls," George spoke with authority. "Grab your purses. We're going down the back way. Linda, lock up the office and take the rest of the day off. Don't go straight home. Here is a hundred dollars. Stop at the mall and go shopping and then take a different way home."

Chapter 5

George and Elle went back into his office and out his private door and down the back hall to the parking garage.

"Where is your car?" George whispered, trying to be quiet, his voice still echoing in the stillness of the parking garage.

"Here. Level twelve." Elle whispered back.

"I'm down on Level six. I'll walk you to your car and then I'll meet you at the Motel 6 in the Wilson Street Mall."

Elle frowned. "Motel 6? Why there? Eeeww!"

"It's where no one would expect us to be. No one would believe you would be caught dead at a Motel 6."

Elle stopped, still frowning. "You make me sound like a snob!"

"Shh! No, no." George took her hand and squeezed it. "I'd never even consider the thought! I just meant you have different requirements for a hotel room!"

"Ugh, that's worse. You make me sound like a call girl!" George was snickering. "No, no, no, that's not what I meant! I just always picture you in a more refined environment!"

Elle sniffed. "Dahling, finally! Now if you could just peel me a grape!" She waved her hand royally and then flicked him in the head. "Well, I guess, if you put it that way, at least it doesn't make me look like an ogre. By the way, why are you way down there on level 6?" Elle whispered.

"It's my back up plan, in case I don't run in the morning. I need the exercise! I can't eat those maple bars and scones every day if don't move around a bit. By the way, today I had none, due to the fact they ended up stuck to Gus' body and were therefore rendered inedible. I need breakfast."

George tucked Elle in her car. "Wait a minute." He shut her car door and went around and got in the passenger side. "Ok, let's go. I want to keep you in my sight. When we get to six, let me out at my car and then I want to follow you to the Motel."

Elle immediately felt better. "Oh Good. Thanks. I'd just as soon not be too far away from you right now." She backed out of her parking place, craned her neck to see what was out there that she might hit, and then pulled forward toward the lower levels.

She stopped behind George's Mustang, and he got out. Before he shut the door, he said, "Ok. I'll follow you and I'll see you at the Motel." He shook his finger at her. "Speed limit. Ok?"

Elle grinned and saluted. She waited for him to get settled and then she sedately continued towards the exit.

Nervously tapping the steering wheel, she waited for her turn to pay. She practically threw her ticket and money at the attendant who deftly caught it all mid-air.

"Whoa, there, pretty lady! Are you in a hurry?" He grinned at her.

"Sorry! Yes, actually I am! So, if you don't mind?" Elle tried smiling back, but her lips were dry and stiff.

He handed back her change and hit the button for the arm to go up, and she scooted on through.

Weaving in and out of traffic, Elle suddenly realized she could be drawing attention to herself, so she adjusted her speed and tried to drive more sedately. She chuckled to herself. As if a red Hummer didn't already turn heads. Oh, how she had wanted this vehicle! She thought back to when her cousin, Jimmy, first went to work at the Hummer/Porsche dealership and the first time she laid eyes on the shiny red Hummer. They teased her because she didn't want a Porsche; she wanted a Hummer. Butch gave her such a hard time. "That's no car for a girl! That's a boy car! People will laugh at you! Don't you care?" NO, she didn't care. She'd stop at the dealership on her way home from shopping or any time she was in the area.

Then the dealership created the obstacle course to show what the Hummer could do. Jimmy took Elle and her sister Mandy out on that course, and Elle was hooked. Entering the course, the Hummer climbed a 24-inch wall, while they hung on for dear life. They climbed over large logs and boulders and up hills, turned a corner with one wheel in the ditch, did a 360 on a dime, and dove down a hill at a ninety-degree angle. Elle tried not to scream but failed. The finale was plowing through a big ditch full of water. It was the most fun, the most terrifying, most amazing twelve minutes she'd ever spent in a vehicle.

It was right up there with flying. Something else she loved. The day she picked up her first paycheck from Qantus she walked into Jimmy's dealership, did the paperwork, and the Hummer was hers. Well, and the bank's.

She continued agonizing about how her life had been upended in the twinkling of an eye. What happened? How did Butch end up being Dr.Jekyll and Mr. Hyde? Why couldn't she have dumped them both before this happened? Why did she hang on for so long? Why did she allow him to torture her? Why had she subjected herself to his endless verbal abuse? Why hadn't she noticed anything peculiar? Why? Why? Gahhh! She knew why, though. There was something about him besides being drop dead gorgeous. He had an aura. Was it pheromones? Whatever it was, it was like a magnet drawing her to him as if she had been a gob of metal. That man could sweet talk the paint off the wall.

She had met Butch in one of the bars in the Portland airport. She had been hired by Qantus right out of flight attendant school, so she enjoyed her jaunts to and from the few cities in the United States where Qantus was available: Atlanta, Boston, Chicago, Honolulu, Dallas, Los Angeles, New York, San Francisco, Washington, D.C. He was on his way to Las Vegas from Portland. She soon realized he was not shy. They were the only ones in the bar at that moment. He moved closer to her to talk to her, and she was smitten. He looked her in the eye when he was talking, which right away caused her bones to melt. Somehow, he learned a lot about her, but she knew nothing about him. He had her phone number in about three seconds flat. She couldn't wait for him to call. In fact, for the first time in her life she didn't want to fly that day! She wanted to go wherever he was going. From then on, she lived and breathed him. They spent every moment possible together. It wasn't always easy finding spare moments between her work schedule and his travel. She wondered why he traveled so much, but when she asked him, he avoided the subject.

Elle never felt like she was particularly shallow, but Butch was so easy on the eyes she hardly cared what was inside his head. From that luxuriously thick hair, already turning silver, to well-shaped pectorals, to that amazingly lean waist and that tight butt. She did manage to learn he was a high hurdler in high school and college, which would explain those gorgeous thighs. She was in awe of every part of him. He was like Adonis. And those kisses… "Ugh! Shut up, Elle!"

She pulled into the parking lot of the Motel 6 and looked for George's Mustang. "Yah we're really incognito now," she said dryly. "No one will notice a bright red perfectly refurbished (for a mere forty thousand dollars) 1965 Ford Mustang convertible, parked next to a bright red giant Hummer. She grinned. "That's me, go big or go home!"

She turned off the ignition and opened the door and attempted to get out. Oh, seatbelt. She frowned. Note to self: unlatch seat belt BEFORE leaving the car. "Get a grip, girlie!" she whispered, and climbed down.

George was waiting for her. "Are you ok?"

"I guess so. I'm kinda numb. I just can't wrap my head around this."

Butch's voice behind them kicked the fear into full gear. George and Elle's heads spun around in tandem, their shock visible. George put his arm around Elle and pulled her tight against him.

Butch stood in the parking lot. Elle observed him from afar. She had to admit he looked good. Black T-shirt stretched over his muscles, faded blue jeans fit snugly over his beautifully shaped legs, and white running shoes. And those blue eyes.

"What are you doing here?" George glared at him.

"More to the point," Elle also glared at Butch, "HOW did you know we were here?"

He snickered. "Well look at you two! Aren't you all cozy? Just good friends, Elle? Really? Are you two-timing me, Elle? That could get dangerous, you know. I never believed you two were just friends. That was always a load of crap! And as for finding you, I'd have to be deaf, dumb, and blind not to be able to find that big red monstrosity! The astronauts can see it from the moon! I never understood what you were trying to prove with that big ugly man machine!"

Elle's mouth flapped open like a fish. "Well, that was not a bit nice, Butch! You've got quite the mean streak! I've never been unfaithful to you, but just to clarify, you and I are finished! Fini! Fertig! Finalizada! Your belongings are all in trash bags in the living room. You have three days to go get them and be gone out of my life and then I call the police. And by the way, I arranged a restraining order."

"Hold on. Wait a minute! There is no need to go on like that. I'd never hurt you! Would I?" It almost sounded like Butch was whining! Weird.

Elle shot him a look. "Want to see some scars?" She looked at George. "See? He's Jekyll and Hyde! Mr. Mood Swing! I can't stay here. Dr. Jekyll can't know where I am, and besides, Motel 6 makes me feel like a sitting duck."

"Elle!" Butch's voice was loud. "Wait a minute. I need to talk to you -- ALONE."

"No! George is my attorney. I don't keep secrets from him."

"Ok. Fine. I've lost something and it's very valuable. I really need to find it."

"Well, if you weren't such a slob, you might have less trouble keeping track of things."

"I'm looking for a book. A small thin notebook. It has some important notes in it and I can't lose it or my life could be in danger."

"Why would I know anything about that – much less care?"

"Please, Elle, you gotta help me!"

"Oh this is cute. You beat me up one day and beg for help the next! You're a funny guy there, Mr. Hyde!"

"Please, Elle, I'm not kidding. I cannot lose that book!" He sounded frightened. Again, he seemed out of character. This was not like him to beg.

"Ok, Butch, go ahead and go to the house and look for it. And when you're done, take all your trash bags with you and leave the key. And be gone out of my life! You have sucked everything out of me. Poke a fork in me. I'm DONE! Go away!" She held her breath, preparing for blowback.

"Thanks, Elle." Butch walked backwards away from them and as he approached his car, he yelled his thanks one more time. Then he stopped. "Elle!" he called. "Wait!" He started walking back towards Elle and George. Elle gripped George's arm.

Butch said, "Can you just take a few steps away from George for just a moment?"

"Now what?" George let her move away from him.

Butch got closer and lowered his voice. "I'm really sorry about the wall."

Elle just glared at him.

He handed her some cash. "Here's some money to cover the damage. I hope you can forgive me."

Elle didn't look at it. She just took it and shoved it into her purse and sighed. "You know money can't fix all the damage."

Butch frowned. "Well, if you need more, just let me know."

Elle sighed. That went right over his head, she thought. She shook her head. "It's fine." She turned and walked back to where George was standing.

Butch got in his car and rolled the window down. "Thanks, Elle," he called as he roared away in his blue Camaro.

" 'Thanks, Elle?' He's thanking me? Ugh." Elle made a face. "Why is he being so pleasant? It's weird. Is he Jekyll or Hyde now?

"Dr Jekyll is the nice guy. Mr. Hyde is the evil one. So, I guess that last pleasantry was Dr. Jekyll." He took her arm and propelled her back to her car. "We need to find someplace to hide your rig. He's right. It's too noticeable. Follow me. I'm going to figure out where to hide that thing."

Elle frowned. "I think I called Butch the wrong name. Do you think he'll think I was complimenting him?"
George smiled. "I'm pretty sure he wasn't even paying attention. So don't worry about it."

Chapter 6

They got in their cars, and Elle followed George out of the lot and into the traffic. She kept him in view for several minutes and was surprised when he entered the freeway. She dutifully followed all the way to the airport. She continued behind him as he turned into the long-term parking area.

"Good Old George!" She said out loud. "So smart!" She drove around looking for a good place to park and spied a big red van with an empty space beside it. "Perfect!" she thought. She placed her ticket on the dash as instructed, got out and slammed the door. She pressed the door lock on her key fob, heard the buzz that assured her the car was secure and turned to George's waiting vehicle.

She hopped in the Mustang, and they roared out of the lot and onto the freeway. She dug in her bag for her sunglasses and put them on so she could stop squinting in the bright sun. She checked the glove box for something to keep her hair out of her face and pulled out her black scarf.

George had gotten this Mustang, his very first car, the day he turned sixteen. Of course, that day, the car didn't look like it did now. It was treated badly by the previous owner and looked like it was ready for the junk yard. Elle had been the first one to sit gingerly in the passenger seat. She had needed a towel to protect her clothes from whatever had previously occupied it. Some kind of animal she hoped was not still lurking in the darkness below. Since that day, there had been a scarf of hers in his glove box.

George's dad had shaken his head the first time he saw the car. He couldn't believe that heap was what George preferred, but he left it up to George to make the decision. Once George was the proud owner, he began the slow process of turning her into the gleaming beauty she was now. He had lots of help. His little brother, fourteen-year-old Matt, crazy about cars from the day he was born and Elle's little brother, fifteen-year-old Chris, also a car nut, had been thrilled when the broken-down Mustang arrived in the Wendling garage. They were delighted and claimed that 1965 was the perfect year for a Mustang.

In fact, even the girls were excited. That was, of course, after they were past the state of disgust at the condition of the car. Then it had become a family project. George, Matt, and Chris spent hours visiting detailers and repair shops. Matt and Chris took a new interest in auto mechanics at their high school. YouTube took priority over Facebook and movies.

The boys worked hard all summer and all through George's senior year. It wasn't finished when George had to leave for university in the fall, but the younger boys promised they would keep working and take good care of it. George came home weekends as often as he could, and the car steadily morphed into a drivable piece of machinery. George was due to return to school the following September when it was finally finished. Both families were present at the unveiling. They celebrated with a barbecue. There wasn't a dry eye in the Wendling back yard that evening.

Elle brought the scarf out of the glove box, tied it on her head, added her Jackie sunglasses and looked over at George. He was smiling.

"How many other girls have worn this scarf?" Elle teased. She was thinking, "Please say none," since she was grossed out at the thought of anyone else wearing it.

"Are you kidding? No woman is allowed to sit in that seat, let alone wear that scarf!"

"Why, George! Are you still carrying a torch for me?"

"That's none of your business! Can we please concentrate on the problem at hand?"

"Oh! Yes! Of course! So sorry!"

"So, we need to find a hotel and you need to check in with a fake name and stay there. Don't leave the room for any reason. But first I need food."

Keeping one eye on his rear-view mirror George drove the speed limit and took the downtown exit. He wound his way around the business district and then turned back down towards the cluster of shops and restaurants and pulled into the McDonald's drive thru. "Elle, do you want anything? It's too late for breakfast. McNuggets?"

Elle watched the video in her head. Her bad self arguing with her good self. She wondered who would win this time. Five, four, three, two, one, "I'll have a Southwest Salad please." She decided not to confess she had already been at McDonalds earlier that morning. "And a large diet coke, please." She had just finished reading "The Five Second Rule" by Mel Robbins and she was trying to use the tools to organize her life. She needed to be better about her health, but it was hard when she was gone from home so much.

When it was George's turn to order he repeated Elle's request and added a double quarter pounder meal, go large, with diet coke. They pulled up to the window and George handed his card to the kid, who took payment and handed it back along with the receipt. They moved forward and gladly received the two drinks which he handed to Elle and then the bag which he also handed to Elle. She held everything while he drove a few blocks to a near-by park. They pulled into a spot in the lot and left the car to go and sit at a picnic table.
Elle chewed thoughtfully. "I'm so glad that book is in your safe! That thing is dangerous."

George carefully opened his double quarter pounder, lifted the top bun, and managed the great art of arranging fries over the cheese. He patted the bun down over the fries and said, "I wonder what will happen to Butch if he can't find the book. How bad are these characters? Who do they work for? How high up the food chain is he or how low is he?"

Elle squirted more dressing on her salad. "I don't even want to think about that. But he can't blame anyone else for his stupidity. He made choices and now he is reaping the consequences."

A mom and some kids arrived with a dog and a soccer ball. Elle felt content sitting at the table with George on this beautiful sunny day. She watched the kids and thought about how someday she'd have a husband and kids and maybe a dog.

The sun shone through the trees making filigree pictures on the table. George put his finger on the imaginary décor. "What do you know about Butch? Where did he come from? Where is his family?"

Elle sighed. "He never talks about family. If I ask him, he just says 'We never speak,' so he's obviously estranged from them. That could be why he's so crotchety sometimes. He must have anger issues."

"That would do it. He strikes me as someone who has always done just what he wanted and damn the consequences. That kind of a kid never had any boundaries."

Elle admired George's perceptive analysis. "Well, he never was very good at having any respect for other people, or their belongings. I can't count the number of times I asked him not to put red towels with black towels in the washing machine. It was like talking to the wall. I'm constantly picking red fuzz off the black towels and black fuzz off the red towels."

George feigned horror. "Oh no, your precious black and red towels? The cad!"

Elle rolled her eyes. "Oh, shut up. You are just hilarious!"

George was still laughing while she started gathering up all the trash and putting it in the bag. "Are you finished? Do you want to go?"

George drank the last of his soda and tossed his cup in the bag. "Yah, let's go." He spied a trash can nearby, so he took the bag over and dropped it in.

Back in the car, George pulled out into the traffic and drove around the downtown area looking for a hotel. Eventually he turned into the lot of the River's Edge Hotel and found a place to park.

They walked in and were greeted by the man at the desk. They tried to register Elle with her fake name, but the desk clerk said they couldn't because he needed valid ID with a credit card. George told the clerk he'd pay, but Elle pulled out some cash from her bag and handed it over and the clerk accepted it. Elle wanted Amelia Earhart for her fake name, but George said that was too obvious. They decided on Billie Gondorff. George knew it was useless to try to talk her out of it since the Sting was one of her favorite movies. The desk clerk frowned and secretly rolled his eyes, but since she paid in cash, he allowed her to use her fantasy name.

At last, they were high up in the hotel in a room overlooking the beautiful Willamette River. George pulled out his cell phone and punched some numbers.

"Extension 4041 please. Thank you... Jack? Oh, good, you're there. I have a huge favor. What? Yes, a really big favor. Yes, big enough for food...Whatever you want. Sure! The Pineapple Express at Dick's Primal Burger. So, anyway, you know the men that burst in this morning with guns blazing? I think they're connected to Elle's ex, Butch. But I need names and soon. Yes. So, here's my question. Is there any way you can legally tell me the results? I don't know how long before it will filter down to us through channels. I don't want you to do something against the rules. Don't get fired! Ok. Thanks. Dick's Primal. Soon. Thanks, man!"

Elle felt safe for the moment, but George didn't really want to leave her. They sat in overstuffed chairs strategically arranged so the occupants could enjoy the restorative tranquility of the river. The idea being guests could relax, allow the stress of the day to fade, and soak up the spectacular view. But the stress of the day wasn't fading. They were both wound tight.

There was a loud knock at the door. "Room service!" said a voice.

They looked at each other. "Elle, did you--?"

"NO! I didn't! Did you--?"

"NO! I didn't either!"

Chapter 7

George and Elle sat rigidly in their chairs. No one was supposed to know where they were! Whoever was at the door knocked again. Again, they heard the words, "Room Service!"

George tiptoed to the door. He put his whole weight against it, prepared for a body to bulldoze into the room, and then opened it just a crack. "We didn't order any room service!"

He widened the crack to see a uniformed waiter standing there with a tray. He could see the tray with the bottle and two flutes.

"Yes sir, I know! Standard procedure for all of our guests when they arrive. Compliments of the house."

George reached in his pocket for some bills and opened the door just a bit further. He thanked the server, handed him the bills and told him to set the tray down on the floor in front of the door.

"Elle, come over here and keep your eye on the hallway, while I bring this in."

Elle obeyed. George set the tray on the table and went back to assure himself the door was locked up tight.

"We're not going to drink that, are we? In the first place, it's too early." She turned the bottle upside down. A drop of liquid landed on the tray. Then another one. She looked over at George, who was staring at the drops on the tray. "And in the second place…"

They both stared at the drops landing on the tray.

George finally said, "Condensation?"

Elle replied, "Faulty manufacturing?"

George took the bottle and set it in the sink in the kitchenette. "What were you saying?"

Elle said, "Oh. I was just about to say I just realized I have nothing! No toothbrush, no clothes!"

"I'll go down to the gift shop and get you some stuff. Would you be ok by yourself for just a short time?"

She smiled at him. "I think so. Just don't be gone long. I'm so sorry I've dragged you into this mess. You've been so great and so patient. I'll be ok. Just be careful."

"Elle, you know how I feel about you. You know I'd do anything for you. I'll stand by you. Remember that. And don't worry. I'm not going to force you to love me back. I'm just glad to hang with you."

"George, you know why I hesitate. I don't have much of a track record. What if it doesn't work out? I'd lose my best friend and I'd die."

"It's ok, Elle, I'll take what I can get. Don't worry but consider this. It's as if we've been together for twenty-seven years, right? We've been a huge part of each other's lives from the day we were born. You don't want to divorce me yet, do you?"

Elle grinned. "You really are the best, so I have to say never!"

"I knew that." He chortled wickedly and grabbed the room key. "Wait. I think we should have some kind of a safe word. Like a word you say to me if things are not right. How about 'black coffee?' Neither of us like it plain black so that should be something that would be easy to remember, right? So if I call you and you say that to me I'll know to call the police. OK?"

Elle laughed. "Ok. That works for me. I guess it's easy enough to make someone imagine that you're just calling to see if I need anything, right?"

"Right." George pointed his finger at her. "Don't open the door to anyone, for any reason, no matter what they say. I'll be back," he said, Terminator style. "And flip the safety latch after I leave."

Elle chuckled. "OK, Arnold!" she replied in that same tone.

George shut the door on his way out. She could hear him whistling down the hall.

Hearing the voice of her sister, Mandy, in her head, 'Don't touch the bedspread in a hotel!' Elle pulled back the bed spread/comforter of the nearest of the two queen size beds and yanked off the blanket underneath. "Hmmm... soft!" she thought, "and beautiful sheets! They look like bamboo. How nice!" Wrapped in her cozy shroud, she silently moved toward the door, quickly flipped the latch, then returned to the easy chair. Reverting to habit, she sat sideways in the chair, kicked off her flip flops and pulled her bare feet up under her. Her phone rang. She saw it was George. Chuckling, she pressed the answer button.

"Hi! You barely left here!"

George replied, "I just made it to the lobby. Just checking. Everything ok?"

"Yup! Everything is A-ok."

"Ok. See you in a few."

She settled back in her chair, snuggled up in the blanket again and lazily focused again on the river. A yacht floated lazily by, and she dozed.

She was bolted out of her reverie by George's arrival. He knocked to the tune of "Shave and a haircut" and Elle flew to the door. She let him in after she heard his voice, and he entered the room loaded with several shopping bags.

"Look what I brought you! See if these are ok."

Elle was laughing. "You are the speediest shopper I have ever met!

He emptied the bags out onto the bed. Elle watched as the items tumbled out: black yoga pants, black and white shimmery tunic top, black velvet hair band with a jewel on one side, one package of underwear, an oversized bright red T-shirt, a bag of some sort of chocolate, two bottles of diet Pepsi, toothbrush, toothpaste, deodorant, shampoo, conditioner, comb, brush, hairdryer, and a smaller bag of objects. Elle looked in the bag of chocolate.

"Ohhh! Are these maple truffles? Yum! And what's in this bag? Oh, George, mascara? Blush? Lipstick?" She was laughing. "You know the hotel room probably has a hair dryer? But, oh, George, you are an angel!"

George grinned. "I know that. I'm relieved to know YOU know that! Sorry they didn't have any Fifth Avenues."

Elle felt an unusual surge of love for this guy. She'd always loved him, but like a brother. They had been best friends since childhood. He'd always been there for her at the end of every failed relationship. She'd always shied away from a romance with him because, like she explained to him, there was always the possibility of it turning out badly and that would just devastate both families. And she'd die without George in her life. She mentally smacked herself in the head and told herself to shut up.

George turned on the television. "Wanna see some Mariners?" He flopped on to one of the queen beds.

Elle looked over at him. "Don't lay on the spread! Throw it off!"

George sighed and rolled off the bed. He gathered up the spread and tossed it over onto the couch. Then he resumed his position on the bed. He grinned. "Any more Mandyisms?"

Elle chuckled. "Yes, the floor is poison."
George's voice took on a more serious tone. "Are you ok, Elle?"

She smiled at him. "You are working overtime to make sure, aren't you?"

They spent the afternoon being lazy and watching baseball. Towards evening George felt his stomach. "Do you hear those rumblings? I'm starving! How about some room service? Or a pizza? What will you have mademoiselle? I'm at your service."

"Uhh... I think Pizza! Yes! Pizza!"

George pulled out his cell phone. Then he stopped. "Hmm… Maybe the landline… I dunno. Would these guys be smart enough to try to track us through our cell phones? And then again, what's the point? We'd have to take the batteries out, which would be a pain. I doubt they would even know where to begin to find us that way." He stood still a minute debating. Finally, he looked up the number on his cell and made the call. Stuffed crust pepperoni and olive, bread sticks, and giant chocolate chip cookie ordered, he ended the call and tucked his phone back in his pocket.

"It's no big deal. We're in this together. Even if we weren't, we still would be."

Elle grinned. "I can't believe I get that, but I do!" George dutifully pulled the bedspread off the other bed and threw it onto the couch and then stretched out with the remote and the Mariners. Elle sat on what had developed into her bed and looked at all her treasures from George's shopping spree. She tried on the hairband and padded over to the bathroom to admire it.

A loud knock on the door froze them into silence. "Oh," George whispered, "pizza… But just to be safe…" he sat up and grabbed an unopened sack from the pile on the bed and pulled out what looked like a gun, then tiptoed to the door.

"George!" Elle shrieked.

"Shhhhhh!" George hissed. "It's just a taser!" He put his ear to the door and listened. "Who is it?"

"Pizza!" came the response.

George flung the door open, and three men blew like a hurricane into the room.

Chapter 8

Elle screamed and George landed on the floor squeezing the taser trigger with his eyes shut. When George opened his eyes, he had a broad view of the ceiling and realized he was still on the floor. Mutt, that same tall gun-toting guy from the office, was inches away, also on the floor, doing the robotic dance one does when one receives 50,000 volts to the solar plexus. Jeff was staring down at him in horror. Butch was kneeling on the floor attempting to breathe life back into the pizza which was permanently attached to the inside cover of the box. Elle was on the floor on the other side of the bed.

"You've killed him!" Jeff grabbed George by the collar of his shirt, shook him, bouncing his head on the floor, and screamed again down into his face, "You've killed him!"

His face closer to that nefarious pipsqueak than he cared, George got a direct whiff of some really bad breath and felt his stomach lurch. He turned his head to the side and gasped for a pocket of fresh air. He pushed Jeff away and said disgustedly, 'He's not going to die!"

"He might wet his pants though, and what a tragedy that would be." Elle oozed sarcasm. She looked over at Butch. "What are you doing here, you freak? How did you get our pizza? Is that our pizza? How did you find us? What have you done with the delivery guy? Why are you here? Well? Answer me!"

"I'm starving! I need food!" There was that whine again. Elle was sure Butch must be schizophrenic. And this was his baby persona, never mind Jekyll and Hyde.

She gave Butch a death look. "You idiot!" It had been a while since she was this furious. "Answer me! What are you even doing here and do you have any clue what is going on in this room right now?"

George managed to get to his feet and headed over to where Butch was still trying to save the pizza. He grabbed a fist full of Butch's shirt and yanked him to a standing position. "Man, you have caused more trouble for more people in one day than Attila the Hun did in his whole career! What is the matter with you? Do you have any inkling of how much trouble you are in??"

Butch stepped back and slapped George's hand off his shirt. "It's none of your business, Buster. Stay out of the this! Who do you think you are, anyway? Elle is MY woman, not YOURS!" Elle's head popped up. "NO, I'm not! As of Wednesday morning about 1:30 am I AM NOT YOUR WOMAN! Actually, I haven't been your woman for some time now!" She pointed her finger at Butch. "And George and I have both been sucked down into your depravity because of your foolishness, Butch, and he's right. You are in deep doo doo mister."

Mutt's sizzling had finally come to an end. He lay on the floor looking drugged. Jeff was angry. "Enough of the chatter," he bellowed. "This is the end of the road for all of you! Give us the black book and do it right now! All of you get over to that side of the room. Move! Who has the book? I'm asking for the last time! I'm going to count to ten and then Butch gets one in the head!"

Butch put his hand up. "Can I ask one question?" Elle and George simultaneously looked at each other and rolled their eyes. Elle wondered if Butch could get any stupider.

Jeff sighed. "What?"

Butch took a step forward. "Can we speak in private? Please?"

Jeff sighed again. "Ok but make it snappy!" Butch motioned for him to step into the bathroom. Jeff handed his gun to Mutt and told him to keep an eye on the others and followed Butch in and the door went shut.

In the bathroom, Butch said, "I think I can get Elle to talk. But if we make her mad or scare her, she won't want to help us. I know she secretly still loves me, and I can sweet talk her and get information from her. But you have to back off. If you don't, she will get mad and do something stupid. And if you kill them, we'll never know where it is, ever. Get it?"

Jeff glared at Butch. "Fine. But if you're wrong, YOUR life is over. Get it?"

Butch swallowed, nodded, and opened the door. Nothing had changed. Relieved, Butch announced that they had come to an understanding. Jeff patted Butch on the back, a bit harder than necessary, and Butch coughed.

"Yah, a BIG understanding! Come on, Tony, we're leaving."
"Wait!" George said loudly. Everyone stopped and looked at him. "Don't you want the darts removed from your chest?"
Mutt showed a yellowed toothy grin. "I already pulled them out, see?"

"Lord, have mercy." Elle gaped at Mutt.

"Uh, are you ok?" George kept his distance, but he looked worriedly at Mutt's torso. "Are you bleeding?"

Mutt cackled again. Elle rolled her eyes.

George said, "Uh, those darts should be removed by a medical professional."

Jeff was getting irritated. "He's fine!" He looked at Mutt. "Well? ARE you bleeding?"

Mutt unbuttoned his shirt and displayed his bare chest. Other than three or four hairs and a mole, there were two brown spots that looked like burns. "See? I'm fine just a bit burned!" again the toothy grin.

Elle rolled her eyes and wondered if he might be dumber than Butch. Mutt's laugh was starting to sound like Homer Simpson. Jeff herded the other two out into the hall and slammed the door. Elle watched shrimpy little Jeff steer the two big guys like some mini cowboy and thought to herself, "Yup. Dumb, Dumber, Dumbest."

George and Elle were finally alone. George whispered, "Did you hear that?"

Elle flopped down on the bed. She was sweating. "Whew! I didn't think we were going to make it that time! Hear what?"

George flopped down on the other bed. "The big guy called the shrimpy guy Tony! That's a clue! I'll call Jack in the morning and see if he knows anything. Also, I gotta call Gus and just make sure he's ok. In fact…" He pulled out his cell and dialed. "Linda? Oh good. You're home. Just checking in. Everything ok? Any messages?" He listened and said 'ok' several times and 'take care of yourself' and 'see you tomorrow' and hung up.

"They found my client, and Jack called, and an FBI agent called for an appointment."

"FBI agent? Really? I wonder what that's about."

"We'll know soon enough. I'm supposed to see him as soon as I'm out of court tomorrow morning."

George stood up and went over to the table to inspect the pizza. "I wonder if this is edible."

"Well, it was really never out of the box, was it? Just smashed to the lid? But. Uh. Handled by Butch. Ick." Elle stood beside him, observing with distaste.

"I'm starving. It's been ages since my last meal. Can we just get room service?"

Elle was immediately solicitous. "You poor thing. Yes! Of course! Order away!"

George got on the phone and ordered enough to feed a third world country. He hung up and grinned. "The feast is on its way!" Elle yawned. "Are you spending the night?"

"Yes. I think I should. I'll leave early in the morning and go home go for a run, especially since I've eaten so much junk, and shower before court. I hate to leave you alone. Don't worry. I promise to behave."

"Of course, you do. You know I can still take you."

"Maybe not. I've been working out. Check out these guns!"

Elle yawned again. "You keep saying that. Maybe another time."

"Any time you're ready, you're on." George paced back and forth waiting for the food. He had found a baseball game to watch so he'd stop occasionally to spend a few minutes standing in front of the television, then it was back to pacing.

Elle stopped him pacing for a moment. "I just remembered. Did you tell Gus you were out of the office all week?"

"Yes. I told him I'd be out all week except for today. Was that just today? Seems years ago."

A knock on the door was a joyful sound and George went to the door. He prepared himself once again just in case. "Who is it?"

"Room service!"

Chapter 9

"Yeah," he thought, "I've heard that before." He opened the door a crack and observed two waiters with large trays of food. He dug in his pocket for some cash and enlarged the crack. In déjà vu fashion, he handed out the cash and told them to put it all on the floor in front of the door. He watched them walk down the hall and into the elevator. Another minute passed and he opened the door and brought the food in. He shut the door and locked it.

Elle's eyebrows disappeared under her bangs. "How long were you planning on staying in this room??" She surveyed the landscape. Two double cheeseburgers, two large plates of fries, two milkshakes, two sodas, two large pieces of cheesecake, and a hot fudge sundae. "...and a partridge in a pear tree," she sang.

"Very funny," George managed to say around a mouthful of cheeseburger. Elle joined him at the table and dug into the fries before they could get cold.

They spent the rest of the evening watching baseball and dozing. George half-heartedly attempted to work on a brief he was writing. During a commercial, Elle looked over at George.

"Did you know that Wikopedia describes Mutt as a tall, dimwitted racetrack character—a fanatic horse-race gambler who is motivated by greed' and Jeff as a 'half-pint inmate of an insane asylum who shares his passion for horseracing?'

George responded with an eye roll.

Friday morning Elle opened her eyes to George's face close to hers. She analyzed the situation and realized that George was attempting to say goodbye.

"Elle?"

"Uh... yes... I'm up. Sort of."

George stood up. "I'm leaving to go home and take a shower and get fresh clothes and then I'm going to go to the office just for a little while and then I'll be back. Remember the safe word? Are you ok being alone for a bit?

Elle lay back on the pillows. "Yes. I'll be ok. You don't have to call me every thirty minutes. Once per hour will be ok."

"Ok. Get up and lock me out."

She followed him to the door, locked it behind him and connected the safety latch. Then she pulled a chair from the dining area and leaned it against the door with door handle over the top of the chair. "That should at least slow him down, whoever 'him' is," she said out loud. Then she went and got a band aid out of her purse and taped it across the peep hole. She stood trying to remember the article she read online about safety precautions in a hotel room. She checked off choosing a room above second floor. She checked off looking in all the closets when first arriving. She checked off the band aid over the peep hole. She looked around and was surprised to find a door stop in the bottom drawer of the dresser. All the doors had metal ones that were attached. Interesting. Evidently it was a good idea to check dresser drawers. Growing up, her mother never had the kids unpack suitcases. She was worried that things would be forgotten, and she wasn't all that sure about the cleanliness of the inside of the drawers. Elle pushed the doorstop under the door to the hallway and returned the kitchen chair to its place under the door handle. There, she thought. Reasonably secure.

Now that she was wide awake, wondering what she was going to do today, she decided to start with breakfast. She ordered a caramel macchiato and a bagel with cream cheese and wondered how it was that she could even be hungry. She thought about the leftovers from last night still in the fridge and wondered why George didn't have a super-sized belly ache this morning. She chuckled to herself and wondered why she seemed to be wondering a lot lately.

"That's it, boys and girls," she said to the empty room. "We have to stop eating so much! Today we change our ways!"

Breakfast arrived and she cautiously pulled the doorstop away, unlocked and opened the door a crack. She handed out the bills she had retrieved from her purse and told them to put the tray down in front of the door. She waited, in keeping with this newly developed ritual, until the waiter was in the elevator, whisked her tray in, and locked the door. She climbed back into bed, scooted up with her back against the pillows, pulled the covers up over her knees and arranged the tray on her lap.

Her cell phone rang. It was George. She listened and nodded. "Ok. Yes, I am ok. Just get here as soon as you can. Good luck!"

"Lovely," she said to the empty room. "How on earth did the FBI connect to Jack?" She sighed. She supposed she'd know soon enough. She drank her coffee and nibbled at her bagel, but her appetite had faded away. She tossed the half-eaten bagel back on the tray and made herself get up and take a shower.

Dressed in her new clothes, looking in the mirror, she told herself she should marry George for the simple reason he had really great taste and had the uncanny knack of getting the right size. Weird, but wonderful.

She straightened the room and left a twenty-dollar bill on her unmade bed. Ever since she was a server in a busy restaurant when she was in college, she tipped big. She knew how hard it was to work in the service industry. Then she went out and sat on the deck to wait for George.

When George arrived, he told her she was already checked out so they could just leave. They didn't even have to go into the lobby. They could just go into the parking garage from the second floor. He was parked right by the elevator. They put the shopping bags in the trunk, got in the car and headed out.

"Where are we going?" Elle opened the glove box and pulled out her black scarf. She tied the scarf over her blonde curls, added her big black Jackie sunglasses and sat back waiting for George to maneuver the busy downtown traffic.

They merged on to Highway 26 west and headed towards the suburbs. "The FBI agent wants to talk to you so we're going to meet him for lunch." They exited at 185th and sped out to the massive shopping area, then turned on to Evergreen Parkway and eventually came to rest in the parking lot of the Thirsty Lion.

"How did we end up here?" Elle was curious.

"I told him it was your favorite restaurant, and it would go a long way to spur you to cooperate." George looked at her with his usual grin. "Don't worry. I didn't tell him you were a hostile witness or anything like that."

They sat in a corner, not very well lighted, which added to the weirdness of it all. The agent, Dan Carson, was very pleasant and patient. Elle surreptitiously looked him over. Yikes! He was young and drop dead gorgeous! Who knew George Clooney had a brother? She mentally smacked herself in the head and ordered herself to focus on the business at hand. By this time, she was ready to tell him everything that had happened so far. She and George took turns talking and Agent Carson made notes.

The server came to take their drink orders. Elle told the guys the Bloody Marys were to die for. After she said it she wished she hadn't. Now "to die for" had taken on a whole new connotation. Since the agent was on duty, he chose soda. George and Elle decided to follow suit. When she came back with the beverages, they were ready to order. The men ordered French Dip sandwiches and Elle ordered a Cobb Salad.

When the food arrived, they took time out to eat but eventually Agent Carson asked George if he had told Elle about what had happened in Jack's lab. George shook his head no. So, Agent Carson explained that when Jack had run the fingerprints from the door in George's office, a big warning sign had popped up on the computer saying the information was classified due to an ongoing investigation and to contact the FBI.

Elle stopped chewing. "I have no response to that." She looked at George.

Agent Carson put his hand on Elle's arm. "Don't worry. We'll keep you safe, but I think maybe you should get a hotel one more night. Just playing it safe."

Elle gently slid her arm out from under Agent Carson's hand and gave him a sick smile. "That sounds nice, Agent Carson."

Agent Carson smiled back. "It will be ok. By the way, how long were you and Butch together?"

"Too long. I should have left him years ago."

Agent Carson apologized for getting too personal.

Elle patted her mouth with her napkin and asked to be excused. George asked her if she needed him to go with her. "I think I can make it to the bathroom and back."

As she made her way to the restrooms, suddenly she was grabbed and lifted off the ground and a big hand clamped over her mouth.

Chapter 10

Her gut reaction was to use her heels to repeatedly kick the shins of whoever had hold of her and to reach back behind her head and slap the attacker's head.

"Ouch, Elle! Stop it!" Butch was pleading for mercy. He let her down with a thump. She whipped around to face him with a vicious glare.

"What do you think you're celebrating, you idiot!" she whispered tersely. "You scared the life out of me!"

"I need to talk to you, Elle! I'm in big trouble. If I don't get that black book back, they're going to kill me and dump me in the river! I'm not kidding!"

"Butch, you are so dramatic! Oh? That book I found under the bed?"

"Yes! You didn't look in it, did you?"

"As a matter of fact, I did glance through it."

"Oh, no. You shouldn't have!"

"Whatever on God's green earth are you involved in?" she asked angrily. "You are mixed up in something not good! Why? It boggles the mind!" Elle was hoarse from screaming at him in whispers.

"I needed the money! You cut me off. I need cigarettes, gas for my car, beer, Jack Daniels! Jack and I are best friends!"

Elle's mind flashed to the list in her head. She had finally looked up the symptoms of bipolar disorder and substance abuse was number one. She had come to know that list like her address. The rest of the list rolled through her brain like a bad movie: Erratic behavior, suicidal tendencies, shopping sprees, guilt, pressured speech, depression, mania, inflated ego, and erratic thought patterns. Every single item on that list she had lived with. Some were constant. Others became prominent and then receded. She lived with that pressured speech whenever they were together. He'd talk and never shut up! She couldn't get a word in edgewise and by the time he took a breath she had forgotten what she wanted to say. Lately, the thought he might be schizophrenic had flitted through her mind.

Elle rolled her eyes. "Why can't you get a job like normal people? Why do you have to do whatever it is you are doing? Your black book is a bunch of gobbledygook, but it doesn't look good!"

Butch's grip tightened on her arms. "Elle! I owe people a lot of money! A lot of money! I can't get a "normal" job! I don't have time!"

Elle wrenched herself out of Butch's reach. "Butch, first of all, STOP GAMBLING! And secondly, I see what the problem is. I'm speaking in English and you're listening in STUPID!"

"What about the book? And by the way, where is my cash?"

She wanted to say, "What cash?" but that might be dangerous given the state he was in already.

"I'll call you and set up a meeting. Now, go away!" She turned on her heel and speed walked down the hall to the restroom. When she returned to the table, both men looked at her and two sets of eyebrows went up slightly. George asked her if she was ok, and she told him about the surprise visitor.

Agent Carson frowned. "We should pick him up. And Elle, I really think I should have the book. You are not safe with it floating around out there. It might help us get to the root of the problem. We may only be looking at the tip of the iceberg."

"It's in George's safe in his office." Elle looked at George. He was staring at her upper arms and frowning. But all he did was nod his head. She looked down at her right arm and her eyes widened. Both arms bore the perfect reddened imprint of Butch's hands.

Agent Carson also observing the reddened arms, turned to George. "Can we arrange to go there and get it?"

George forced himself to look over at Agent Carson. "I'd like that thing to be out of my safe. I'll feel a lot better. Let's go now."

George paid the bill over the half-hearted protests of the agent, and they headed to their cars in the parking lot. Elle got in with George, overwhelmed with a weird sense of dread. She felt the hair on the back of her neck stand up. "Let's hurry, George."

George stepped on the gas and all thousand gleaming Mustang Mach 1 GT 500 horses galloped away. The traffic was the usual heavy midday bumper to bumper, and the day was warm. Elle pressed the button and watched her window move gently down, but as the gas fumes from surrounding vehicles rolled in she decided there was no fresh air to be had so she rolled her window back up and opted for some air conditioning.

They arrived at George's building and entered the parking garage, which Elle noticed seemed very empty this time of day. She decided everyone had gone to lunch or taken the rest of the day off. They chose a space near the door on the twelfth floor. The slams of the car doors echoed around the empty building. Elle absently counted. One, two, three, four. Four? Doors slamming should only be three. George, Elle, Agent Carson. Why a fourth door? She stayed close to George.

Since Wendling & Wickersham had the entire 12th floor, their office had a private entrance for all the office staff. Then there was also the public entrance, which, at the moment, had the big rolling steel gates across the front. Agent Carson met them at the private entrance to the office. George tapped the numbers on the key pad and opened the door. Elle followed George. The agent made sure the door was secure behind them.

George stopped and held up his hand.

Elle whispered, "George, what's the matter?"

"Someone has been in here." He whispered back. "Do you smell that? Fresh cigarette."

Elle grabbed George's arm. "Don't go in there!" She was visibly frightened. George turned and very gently patted her shoulder and motioned for her to stay put and for the agent to come with him. Then he stopped.

"Wait!" Elle grabbed George's sleeve. "I am not waiting here by myself! I'm coming with you!"

George frowned. Then he motioned for her to be quiet and turned to the agent.

"I think I will bow to the professional. Would you like to go first?"

"Yes, George," Carson whispered. "But first, I could lose my job for what I'm about to do." He reached inside his jacket and pulled his Glock out of the holster. Then he bent down and pulled out a Sig from his ankle holster and handed it to George.

George gave him the thumbs up. "Who am I going to tell?" He unlocked the door, and the men began a methodical search of the rest of the office. Elle followed quietly, straining her ears for any unusual sounds.

They checked the dads' offices, and the main lobby. In each one, the floor was littered with papers and file folders and overturned furniture. Drawers hung drunkenly askew.

George and the agent had saved George's private suite behind his office for last, hoping the casual observer wouldn't even have noticed the door. It had been designed to be just that – barely noticeable. George let Agent Carson go first. The agent quietly opened the door a crack. Then a bit more. There was silence. He stuck his gun in and then his head. Then the rest of him disappeared inside. A minute passed. Then he stepped back out and shut the door.

"George, before we go in, maybe you should take Elle straight out to the desk in the lobby and have her sit down."

Elle balked. "No, I don't want to be relegated anywhere! What is going on?" Her hackles were up in defiance.

Agent Carson looked at George. "There is a body on the floor in there."

Chapter 11

Elle covered her mouth in horror. She removed her hand to say, "A d-d-dead b-b-body? Who is it?"

Agent Carson opened the door again. "George, you go have a look. I'll stay with Elle. I'm sure you know very well not to touch anything, although your fingerprints, as well as Elle's, are everywhere since this is your office.

George entered his private office. When he reappeared, he put his arm around Elle and held her close. "It's Butch," he said to the top of her head.

Elle stood in the curve of George's arm, stunned speechless. She felt the room start to spin and turn blue. She clutched George's shirt. "I think I need to sit down," she whispered. Her knees did not feel reliable. George walked her out to the lobby and put her in an overstuffed chair. She leaned back, closing her eyes.

Butch was dead. Dead.

She couldn't believe it. Dead.

Did she feel bad? She didn't know.

Was she glad? No!

Shocked. Her brain was trying to comprehend it.

She was numb.

Maybe that's what being in shock was.

Was she sad for Butch? She didn't know.

Did she feel relief? That was brutal, but, yes, maybe.

Should she be crying? She felt guilty for not crying.

Guilt. She felt guilty for not being honest with him.

She should have ended it a long time ago.

Guilt.

Guilty. Her eyes flew open. She sat up straight.

Was it her fault that Butch was dead?

Was it because she kept the book?

O dear Lord in Heaven!

No. She refused to go down that road.

She did so much for him, and he treated her badly.

She couldn't control him. Not ever!

Nope. She had nothing left.

Except guilt.

Every ounce of emotion was gone.

He had sucked that all out of her years ago. Verbal abuse, mood swings, the constant demand for what pleased him. All of her energy had been used up a long time ago. She didn't have anything left, except a shriveled-up heart.

"I should look at him," she said to herself. She needed to know if he was really dead. So, when George came to check on her, against his better judgment, he took her to see Butch. They let her in the room. She looked around at the disaster then down at Butch's body. He was spread-eagled face down on the carpet. There was a large blood-soaked mass on his back.

She looked at George. "They shot him in the back. How low can they be?" She looked sadly at those beautiful thighs thinking about how she had always teased him about how she enjoyed watching him walk away. It occurred to her how ironic that statement was. But then his gut-wrenching words followed by the punch to the sternum came to the surface of her mind once again. She turned her back, walked out through George's office to the lobby and sat down in Linda's chair. She didn't feel anything. Not joy. Not sadness. Just nothingness.

George waited while Agent Carson made the necessary phone calls. Local homicide department. His FBI superiors. The agent turned to George. "Did you recognize him even though he was face down?"

George nodded. "Unfortunately. He's been the burr under my saddle for far too long." The agent smiled. "Do you know his next of kin?"

George shook his head. "He never told Elle anything about his family or even where he was from." George sighed. "He was careful not to share anything personal. I need to go check on her anyway." George went off in search of Elle. He found her, still in Linda's chair, staring into space.

"Elle," he said gently.

She turned to meet his eyes. "Are they coming to take him away?"

"Yes. Agent Carson made the phone calls. You're going to have to wait and answer questions. Are you up to that?"

"Sure. I'm ok. I'm just tired. Stunned. It all feels so surreal."

George went out to unlock the front door and raise the gate. And just in time. The elevator opened and spilled out what he assumed to be detectives, forensics and the coroner. He held the door open for everyone, spotting his friend Jack in the group. They made eye contact and he stayed back so he could talk to George. They shook hands and he asked if it was one of the guys he printed.

"No, it's actually Elle's ex."

"Oh no. How is she?"

"She is surprisingly ok. He was a brute. She finally had all she could take."

"Ok. Good for her. I'd better get. Let's catch up later." He hurried after his colleagues.

George watched from the doorway as Jack stopped to talk to one of the detectives. He pointed to George and the detective approached him.

"I'm looking for Elle." George motioned him through the door pointing to Elle.

She attempted a weary smile at the detective as he pulled up a chair and dug in his pocket for his notebook.

In her numbed state, Elle answered all of his questions the best she could. As she talked, she could feel the exhaustion creep slowly through her body. She felt like a bag of wet cement. Her mind drifted. She couldn't wrap her head around the fact that Butch was gone forever. Really gone. Life with Butch was really over. He was gone. No more restraining orders. No more screaming matches. Never again would he yell obscenities in her face. No more sleepless nights when he was so hyped up he spent all night in the kitchen cooking food he'd never eat. No more would he run the washing machine with three items of clothing. Or run the dishwasher for a glass and a plate. No more stinking up the shed smoking pot. No more cigarette butts everywhere. Never again would he take her car and forget to pick her up. She guessed it was good that he had made some money, albeit possibly illegal, so he could get a car of his own.

The detective patted her on the shoulder. He handed her his card, and told her she could go, reminding her to go downtown and sign her statement. She looked around for George. He was in his office, surveying he disaster. The forensic team had finished, and they were packing up. There was black dust on doorknobs, door jams, and flat surfaces everywhere. The coroner's team came out of the private suite with the body, and Elle turned her back. She just couldn't watch.

George came to stand with her. "Are you ok?" She nodded and yawned. He looked around at the mess and watched the last of the crime team head for the elevators. He followed them into the hallway and then locked the door, lowered the gate, and returned to his office.

He put an arm around Elle and said, "Let's go." She gladly went.

She felt better when they closed the door to the office behind them and entered the parking garage. They got into the Mustang and headed out to find a place to sleep. Elle felt like it was the middle of the night, but it was just early evening. What a day! In just a few minutes a hotel loomed into view and George pulled into the parking lot and found a place to park. They sat there in silence for a few minutes.

George looked over at Elle. "How are you doing?"

She smiled sadly. "I'm ok. Just numb. Can't believe he's dead, but--"

George patted her arm. "But what?"

Elle stared straight ahead. "It's my fault Butch was able to get in your office." A tear rolled down her cheek.

"Why do you say that?" George put his hand on her arm. "Elle? What are you talking about?"

"One day when he was with me, and we came in to see you he watched me type the numbers on the keypad. Usually, I put my other hand up over the pad if he's with me. I didn't even think until he said it might come in handy to have those numbers. I meant to tell you to change the code after that. It just went right out of my head." More tears flowed. "Oh, George, I've rained down so much horror on you! How can you ever forgive me?"

George was trying not to tear up along with her. He swallowed. He put his hand up to her chin and brought her face around to his. He looked her in the eye. "I love you. But let's set that aside for now. I'm your best friend. We're in this together –up to our necks – but we're in this together. I wouldn't want it any other way! Ok?" He pinched her cheek. "Let's go, ok?"

She nodded and opened the car door. George retrieved their belongings, locked the car, took Elle's arm, and aimed her towards the lobby. They requested a room on the highest floor possible, ignoring the inquisitive look on the desk clerk's face. They also ignored the raised eyebrow when he saw they had no luggage, but as a professional in the service industry, he refrained from commenting. When he saw Elle's shopping bags, he did ask if they had a pleasant day shopping, and they both wearily nodded yes.

In the room, George locked the door, and they both fell onto the beds, Elle on one and George dutifully on the other. Elle told the Mandy voice reminding her about the bedspread to shut up.

Elle raised her head to look at the clock. "Eight o'clock. Is that a.m. or p.m.?" she joked. "Would you care if I took a nap, George? George?" she looked over at the other bed.

George was asleep. So, Elle put her head down and closed her eyes.

The shrill ringing of the telephone shattered the quiet.

Elle, words muffled due to her face in the pillow, asked who would be calling them and told George not to answer.

It kept ringing.

George finally said, "Hello. Oh, yes, that would be fine! Seven would be great. Well, that would be amazing! Thank you! Let's see… Two Caramel Macchiatos, two blueberry scones, two maple bars, and two cranberry orange scones. Thank you so much! That is so kind of you!"

"What was that all about?" Elle's face was still in the pillow.

"The desk clerk said we looked really tired and just wondered if we would need a wake-up call. And then he wondered if we would like to pre-order breakfast. What a nice guy."

"Do I get cranberry orange scones?" Elle lifted her head to get some fresh air.

"Of course. If you ever decide to hate cranberry orange scones, you had better warn me."

"Gotcha." Elle's head flopped back, and the pillow was once again a mass of blonde curls. She had thick hair and when she was upright it was just past her shoulders. So that pillow got good coverage.

George's heart gave a lurch. He loved that girl so much it hurt. He turned on his side, grabbed the other pillow, punched it up, and curled up around it. He shut his eyes and then opened them again. It dawned on him they had missed dinner. Then he shut his eyes and slept. He was dreaming about chopping wood at his grandfather's. This was a common occurrence. His grandparents owned a huge farm, and they had a cavernous fireplace in their spacious high ceilinged living room. From the time he was able to lift an axe, it was his job to keep the firewood piled high. So, any time he was there visiting, which was a lot in the summer, it was his job to keep the fire going. It was a full-time job. He still had the callouses! Chop. Chop. Chop.

The chopping turned into knocking.

Knock. Knock. Knock. There was someone at the door. He raised his head and looked at the clock. Two-fifteen a.m. He rolled off the bed, staggered to the door, and opened it a crack. It was the desk clerk and a uniformed policeman. Scratching his head, George opened the door a few inches more and asked what the matter was. The officer said it would be better if they talked inside the room. Feeling like this was a weird dream, he opened the door and stuck his head out.

He eyed the policeman. "Could this possibly wait until morning?"

The officer shook his head. "No, sir. I'm sorry."

George looked up and down the hall and finally allowed them to enter. The desk clerk told the officer he needed to return to his post. The officer nodded and the clerk disappeared down the hall.

Wondering what was happening, Elle opened her eyes and listened to George's conversation with whoever was out in the hallway. Deciding she had better get up to see what was going on, she reached for her robe and realized she and George were both fully dressed and neither one had bothered to get under the covers. So, she rolled over and scooted up until her back was against the headboard.

The officer stepped in and closed the door. He identified himself as Police Officer Gerald Miller. He fished out his notebook and flipped the current page over to see a notation, looked up and asked both if one of them owned a 1965 Mustang convertible.

"Yes," George nodded. "I do. Why?"

"I'm afraid it was blown up at approximately 1:30 a.m."

Chapter 12

"Did you not hear the explosion?" Officer Miller looked at George. George looked stunned. So, the officer looked at Elle. She had the same stunned look. Neither of them said a word. They were both speechless. George sat down heavily on the edge of Elle's bed, dumbstruck. Elle left her place at the head of the bed, grabbed some tissues from the nightstand and moved over to sit beside him. She wondered if George was angry or trying not to cry. She put her arm around him, and he finally spoke. His voice was tremulous. "Was anyone hurt?"

"Fortunately, no, but as you can imagine, your car is totaled. I'm so sorry."

George, head bowed, elbows on his knees, ran his hands through his ginger hair. Elle was sure he was crying. His head in his hands, he answered the officer with a weak, "Thank you." Elle's heart ached for him. That car was his pride and joy. Looking up at the officer who stood quietly, she asked if there was anything he needed them to do.

"Do you want to come down and take a look before the tow truck comes?

"You'll give us all the information on where they'll take the car?" Elle spoke to the officer, but she was looking at George.

"Yes, it will be towed to the police evidence garage. I'll leave the card here on the table for you. And my card is there as well. I'll need you to come down to the station and give a statement this afternoon if it's possible. Elle thought to herself if she heard the words 'go down to the station and sign a statement' one more time she'd explode.

Elle looked at the top of George's bowed head "Yes, we'll be there. "Thank you."

After the officer left, Elle just sat quietly beside George, letting him quietly deal with this devastating news. When he finally looked up, she saw his red rimmed eyes and knew his heart must be broken. She looked at the clock on the nightstand.

"It's only three o'clock. What can I do for you? You probably need brandy. That's supposed to be good for trauma." She stood up and went over to look in the mini bar. She found a mini bottle of brandy, grabbed a glass and brought it over to George. She poured part of the bottle in the glass.

"Here. Drink this. It should help you feel more human."

George threw it back in one gulp and then sat still while it burned all the way down.

She looked at his face. He looked shell-shocked. "Do you want to try to get some sleep? It's too early to do anything." George stood up and stretched. "I dunno. I guess there's really nothing I can do this time of night. I'll try and see if I can sleep." He moved over to his own designated bed and lay down, again on top of the covers. "Thanks, Elle."

"For what? It's ME that should be begging for forgiveness! I got you into this mess and now your car is demolished!"

"Please, this is not your fault. It's that ass, Butch. He's dead but still causing trouble. I just meant I appreciate your being so solicitous. I hate acting like a baby, but I loved that car." His voice cracked on those last few words, and he stopped.

Elle smiled gently. "I'm just thankful you weren't in it at the time!"

George closed his eyes and tried not to cry, or at least not sob out loud. His body and soul had taken a beating that day and he tried to succumb to its need for rest and repair.

Elle stretched out on her own bed, wondering if she should get up and wash her face and put on her night shirt, but she was too comfortable and drifted off. She slept badly. Most of the night she listened to George, blowing his nose and crying soundlessly. She tossed and turned amidst weird dreams of Butch with distorted facial features yelling at her. Twice she woke up sweating. The second time she made herself get up. There were still ice and lemon slices in the tall glass carafe on the tray arranged on the dresser. She chose one of the glasses and poured herself some cold ice water. She tried to be quiet, but came a voice from the wilderness of George's bed, "Is there enough for me?" His voice was hoarse, his head stuffed up as if he had a cold.

She poured some for George and took it to him. She switched on the lamp and sat on his bed and waited. His eyes were puffy. Nose red from blowing it so much.

"I loved that car. I know it's silly to love inanimate objects, but we had some great times working on it. It's the only car I've ever had!" Then his face crumpled up and his hands went to his face. "How ever am I going to tell the boys?" He bent over, his head on his knees and sobbed out loud."

Elle was trying not to sob out loud, but the tears were streaming down her cheeks. Her heart broke. She wept for George and for Matt and Chris and for the sadness the whole family would feel. She continued to gently pat George's back and handed him more tissues.

"We had a lot of fun, didn't we?" Elle smiled at the memories flowing through her mind. "Summers at the lake. That fun trip to Glacier Park. What a hoot. You put the top up because you thought a bear might jump into the car with us." George smiled sadly.

"I was nineteen. I'd never been that close to a bear. Our dads just chase moose and elk and fish!" George smiled again. He looked at the clock. "What a night. Is it too early to call room service?"

"It's five a.m. We have an order coming at seven. Do you want to order some coffee? I think we have one packet of regular left for this coffee pot, or do you want lattés?

"I need some good coffee." He leaned over to the phone and called the desk and asked for room service.

Elle stood up and went to the large picture window in the sitting room area. The sun was just barely peeking above the horizon. Streaks of pink and blue were beginning their stint across the sky. She yawned. Good thing coffee was on its way.

George pointed the remote at the TV and flipped through channels to ESPN. Elle went out on the balcony to watch the sun begin its daily travels.

Chapter 13

There was a knock on the door. Elle's heart skipped a few beats. She and George both went to the door. George opened it a crack, hair on the back of his neck at attention. He opened the door an inch more and stuck his head out. Face to face with the green coated waiter from room service. The waiter smiled and said, "Good Morning!" George opened the door all the way to let the man and his cart into the room.

The waiter transferred everything from his cart to the table and departed. On the way out, George handed him some bills and told him they had an order due at seven a.m. they could cancel. The waiter promised to take care of that. As soon as the waiter was out of the room, George locked the door. On his way to the breakfast table, he stopped and called the desk to let them know they wouldn't need the wakeup call at seven a.m.

Elle had watched the delivery of the coffee. When more than the coffee arrived, she was amused. "I thought we were just getting coffee now and then breakfast at seven.

There was a complimentary morning newspaper on the table and George sat down and opened one of the coffees and unfolded the paper. Elle joined him, noting the usual breakfast accoutrements. She selected the other coffee and took a drink. "Oh, that is good! And nice and hot! Nectar of the gods!" She raised her coffee cup and he met hers with his cup. "To the King!" they said in unison. He smiled wistfully. Her heart hurt for him.

Saluting the king was a product of their play as children. After he read *A Connecticut Yankee in King Arthur's Court* and watched *The Sword in the Stone* and the many versions of *Robin Hood,* George went through a stage when he was all things Medieval. So when they drank soda, or anything, they always toasted the King. As they grew older, even though Queen Elizabeth was now the reigning monarch, they never bothered to change it to accommodate her.

They sat for a while in sad but companionable silence, drinking coffee, George pretending to read the paper and Elle enjoying the view of the blue sky and the mountains in the distance. She marveled again at how George could stuff himself with two maple bars and two blueberry scones and look so fit. She ate one cranberry orange scone and drank her coffee and was satisfied.

Suddenly, George folded up the newspaper, smacked it on the table and stood up. "As much as I'd like to, I can't sit here all day. We've got stuff to do. We need to get dressed – wait. We ARE dressed. We need some fresh clothes. I'll go home and shower and dress and find you something to wear." He yawned. "Wait. I can't go anywhere. I have no car. How could I possibly have forgotten that?" He gritted his teeth daring the tears to appear. He turned to face Elle. "I'll have to call Linda."

"Have her take you to get my car. You can use it as long as you need to. Come to think of it, we need to find Butch's car. You can drive mine and I'll use Butch's until you decide what kind of a car you want to get."

"Why don't I just drive Butch's car?"

"No. If they see a man driving his car, they may want to shoot him or blow him up just to be sure. NO, bad idea."

George stood still. He was quiet for a minute. Then he turned and looked at Elle.

"No, this is all a bad idea. Driving your car is a mistake and anyone driving Butch's car is a huge mistake. I'm going to have Linda take me to get a rental – something plain and unremarkable. And you should not be seen in public! I think you should just stay here today until we see what's going on."

"In that case, can you get me a book to read? See if you can find the latest Felix Francis. Are you ok to drive?" Elle examined his face from afar. His blue eyes were red rimmed from shed tears. There were circles under them, too. He was pale which made his freckles seem darker. He looked tired. Hard day yesterday followed by a really short night never did much for a person's health. And his hair was even more unruly than usual. His was curly too, and they both had to spray and mousse their hair to prevent frizz.

George talked to his sister and after the barrage of questions about whether they were safe and fed, she agreed to come get him and take him to get a rental. He told her Elle's wishes for clothing and a book to read. On the way she stopped and picked up some clothes for Elle. She had always enjoyed shopping for Elle because Elle only wore black, white, or red with the occasional yellow thrown in for good measure. Her toenails were only painted red. And jewelry was white gold. And that was pretty much that.

Linda stopped at a bookstore and picked up a Felix Francis book with the aid of the clerk and her assurances it was the latest then moved on to Macy's. She found a pair of black jeans with sequins on the pocket, a red boat neck T-shirt with sequins on the left shoulder, and a cute black sweater hoodie in case it got chilly. She eyed some black barefoot sandals with sequins, which she knew Elle would love. She paid for her purchases and was soon on her way to Elle and George.

She pulled up in front of the hotel and called George to tell him she was on her way up. She told the doorman she was just delivering some things and would be right back. Her heels clicking on the shiny hardwood, she slipped into the first elevator that opened and was zooming her way to the top floor.

George opened the door a crack to see who it was and let her in. Elle was sitting cross legged on the bed in yesterday's wrinkled clothes eating her second cranberry orange scone. Linda sat on the bed with her and displayed her purchases. "Are you ok, Sweetie? You've had a rough go."

Elle smiled wearily. "I'm ok. Just numb. I don't know how to feel. Thanks for taking care of me. You and your brother have been so great keeping me in clothes!"

Linda kissed her on the cheek and stood up. "Let's get going, brother o'mine. We have miles and miles to go before I sleep. YOU, on the other hand, apparently don't sleep." George gave her a look and grabbed his jacket.

"Now, Elle, don't open the door to anyone. Just stay here and out of sight. Remember the safe word?"

Elle smiled and saluted him. "Yes sir! I promise!" As soon as they left, she checked to make sure the door was locked, and flipped the hook across for extra safety and put the door stop in place. She crawled back up onto the bed and finished her scone and the last of her caramel macchiato while she lazily checked out all of her new clothes.

Linda was such a great sister – to George. "And to you, girlie," she said to herself. She wondered what it would be like to be married to George. For sure, there would be sanity. That was definitely a plus. She sure didn't have any with Butch. People think women are high maintenance. They never met Butch! She felt her energy disappear just thinking about him. He had sucked her emotions dry. He had drained her soul and left her exhausted.

All those times he'd wake her up in the night and make her go with him for a drive. Ugh! She'd be sobbing in the car. Why couldn't she have stood up to him and told him to go away? She was afraid. That's really why. He was like a loose cannon. She never knew when he'd freak out or have a melt down or kill them both. That's why it was so shocking to discover that black book. She always knew he was unstable and narcissistic and bipolar, so why not schizophrenic? If that was the case, she could certainly see Butch having a personality that functioned as the book implied. It would make perfect sense. But that was a personality she had never met! Someone so devoid of emotion? Someone so devious, so conniving, so rigidly calculating! It boggled the mind.

She thought about going back to sleep, but not knowing when George would get back, she thought she had better be ready when he arrived. So she showered and got dressed in her new clothes and modeled them in front of the mirror. In spite of all the terrible stuff that was going on, she felt loved and spoiled. She should have Linda do all of her shopping!

She tidied up the hotel room, thankful they had brought everything out of the car. She pulled on her new hoodie and slid the balcony doors open.

No wonder they didn't hear anything last night. The usual street noises were non-existent, and the loudest sounds were of the birds flying overhead. She stood out there soaking up the fresh air and letting the early morning breeze lift tufts of her hair and helpfully finish drying the last few tendrils that had escaped the hair dryer.

Knocking on the door put her hackles up. It was too soon for George to be back. It wouldn't be Linda. Room service? Why? Desk Clerk? Why? She decided to take a chance and see who was there. Leaning against the door, as if that would really make any difference at all, she said, "Who is it?"

Chapter 14

Elle waited.

"It's me, Agent Carson." Came the voice.

Elle breathed a sigh of relief and opened the door, smiling. "Come in!"

She motioned to the small living area and sat in one of the overstuffed chairs. He sat close to her on the end of the couch.

"What's happening," she asked. "How did you know where I was?"

Agent Carson chuckled. "Since George is a person of interest in this case, I got the message about his car being blown up." He smiled at her. "You are so beautiful. George is a lucky man."

"Yikes!" Elle thought. "What a weird thing to say. That was not what I was expecting and so unprofessional!"

She gave him a look and said a rather lame thank you.

"Are you guys serious or are you just friends?"

Elle did another mental step backward. This was going down a wrong path.

"Uh. do you have any clue who might have blown up George's car?" She stood up and pretended she needed to stretch her legs. She walked to the kitchen and back and turned to Agent Carson. "Who could it be?"

Agent Carson smiled again. Elle frowned. She wasn't feeling the same vibes from him as she had before. He seemed distant. Different. His smile was rather stiff, and his eyes were a steady cool blue. "It was me," he said with the same cool tone. He stood up.

Elle felt physical pain like a knife to the heart. Suddenly she was furious. And terrified. She hoped the cacophony of emotions zipping through her body didn't show. She turned and casually walked back to the kitchen. She pretended she was getting a drink of water. She reached for a glass and filled it at the sink. She wasn't thirsty but she took a sip of water anyway just to kill some time and then as she was about to return to where she and the agent were standing, she was horrified to discover Agent Carson had followed. She backed up. He took another step forward. Her fists clenched, she willed her brain to be calm, while madly attempting to imagine if there were any sharp knives in a hotel kitchen. She struggled to keep her breathing even while she mentally opened the drawers searching each.

She backed up a few more steps. Again, he followed. He was very close. Elle had never considered herself to be attractive in a sexy way. She had been told she was pretty, but she had never felt the need to flaunt herself to get attention. Besides which, that wasn't the way she wanted to attract the limelight. In fact, she had tried very hard to ignore the animal type behavior she was seeing in Agent Carson. Not only were his advances unwelcome, she felt revolted.

She didn't dare turn her back. She put her hands behind her and took another step. He didn't seem to be in a big hurry. "Well, why would he," she thought, "he probably knows fifty ways to kill someone, even without a weapon. And not even leave a mark."

"Elle, I just need to tell you something."

"W-what?"

"You probably should just let everything go and not pursue the investigation into Butch's death. Just leave it alone. It would be better for everyone."

"What on earth do you mean?" She was shocked.

He smiled that smarmy smile. "It would just be safer for you if you didn't try to solve Butch's murder."

"What do you mean, safer?" Elle was feeling around for the kitchen counter behind her.

Agent Carson took a step closer. "You wouldn't want to end up like Butch, would you?"

Elle's mouth fell open. "Are you threatening me?"

"It's not a threat. It's more like a warning." He put his hand on her cheek.

Elle removed his hand and stepped back until she felt the counter in the small of her back. "I can't believe you are saying this to me! What kind of a detective are you, anyway? Threatening me? Or warning me? Or whatever you call it?"

He leaned towards her. She was starting to feel claustrophobic. "It's better this way. I really don't want you to end up like Butch."

Elle's eyes widened. "What? Of course not! Why would I? I haven't done anything wrong." She frowned. "Why would you say something like that?"

Agent Carson closed the gap between them. "I'm trying to help you, sweetheart!"

Elle blinked. Sweetheart? "Uh, Agent Carson, you're being rather familiar, aren't you?"

Agent Carson 's upper lip curled cementing Elle's revulsion. "Please call me Dan. Elle, you're so cute. I just want to cuddle you up and smother you with kisses!"

"Agent Carson! I can't believe you said that out loud! You are being very unprofessional!" Elle was determined not to let him see how frightened she was. She could feel his breath on her face. The kitchen counter was digging a hole in her back, crushing her ribs.

"You really should cooperate with me," he whispered.

"What are you saying?" She could feel the tears coming. "You—you didn't blow up George's pride and joy!"

"How could I get you to cooperate? I needed leverage!" His eyes bored a hole through her. He was losing the charming façade.

"You couldn't be THAT wicked! Why would you do something like that? You have no idea the pain you have caused!" Elle was standing up straight, leaning away from him as much as she could, all the while trying to decide which way to run.

Right before her eyes, Agent Carson freakishly changed personalities. "There's more," he said slyly. "Wanna hear more?" "What is going on?" Elle asked. The ongoing struggle to keep herself calm was taking its toll. She desperately did not want to cry. She stopped. Her voice just a whisper now "You didn't—you surely didn't kill Butch?" She put her hands on his chest and pushed. "You were so nice! Oh! You just didn't kill Butch, did you? No! You didn't! Why?" Her words were a terse whisper, but her anger was obvious and now the tears were flowing.

Agent Carson's friendly chuckle had turned into a creepy monster whine. "He was getting greedy, Elle. He wanted more money. I can't have people pushing me for more money all the time! And what's this? I thought you wanted to be rid of him!"

"Wait. Why were you giving him money?" Behind her back Elle's fingers met up with the hard surface of the kitchen counter. Standing perfectly still, she tried to quietly get the drawer open, but her body was rammed too hard into the counter. She stopped. He was staring at her. Now, she was calm. She spoke softly, telling him he was mean and hateful. His eyes were on her face. She decided against the knife idea, since she couldn't even get to it. Bad idea. There could be blood and maybe hers.

He just stood there laughing at her. "You're beautiful when you're angry."

She groaned. "That phrase has been overdone. And you haven't answered my question! Why were you giving money to Butch?"

His eyes were still on her face. He wasn't looking anywhere else. His guard was down, and Elle seized the moment. Suddenly she kicked him really hard in the shin.

"Owwwww!" he yelled. "That really hurt, you bitch!" Elle silently agreed. It was her bare foot that had connected with his shin. She hoped she could still walk. Then just to keep him busy, she stomped as hard as she could on his foot.

"Owww! You bitch!"

That was better, she thought. She could do a lot more damage flat footed. She ran to the phone. Keeping Agent Carson in view, she dialed 911.

"What is the nature of your emergency?" the nasal voice asked.

She talked fast. "I need police! I've an intruder in my hotel room!" She gave the name of the hotel and the room number. Agent Carson was hobbling toward her. She held the button down and then dialed zero. Agent Carson grabbed her arm and pulled the phone out of her hand, and it hit the floor with a crash. She was yelling frantically, hoping someone was listening, yelling her room number and that there was an intruder, and she needed security! She also hoped she wasn't yelling at a dial tone.

Agent Carson still had her arm in his tight grasp. He was hurting her. She wished she had something to hit him with. Fully aware that he still had his gun, she decided to go limp and see if he'd loosen up. She eyed the lamp on the end table near the couch. It had a wide shade and a tall thin body with a large base. That was her destination. The tears she had been holding back now flowed full force. She made herself relax as if she was giving up. As she felt the grip on her arm begin to loosen, she put both hands up to her face and turned toward the end table, still sobbing.

He still had her left arm in his grip. Suddenly in one swift move, she grabbed the lamp with her right hand and swung it high so the base made direct contact with the side of his head. He went down like a ton of bricks. She stood over him long enough to see he was unconscious and, ignoring the goose egg growing on the right side of his head, reached into his coat and pulled his Glock from his shoulder holster and his Sig from his ankle holster. She ran in the bedroom and stuck them in an empty dresser drawer. Then she flew to the door and waited desperately, praying it hadn't been a dial tone, for security to arrive. Standing at the door she wondered if she should take a chance and get the phone put back together and call again, but it was on the floor right by Agent Carson. She really didn't want to get that close. She glanced at his head. Blood was oozing from that goose egg. She hadn't thought she had broken the skin, but obviously she was mistaken. "Great." She said aloud. Now they'll throw the book at me for assault and battery!" She anxiously took inventory of the room trying to think of something she could use to tie him up.

There was a hard knock, and then a bass voice boomed out, "Security!" Elle yanked the door open and grabbed the officer's arm.

"Hurry! Hurry! Cuff him! Agent Carson was beginning to wake up. "Hurry, cuff him!"

"What is the matter with him?" the security officer looked puzzled.

"He came after me and I hit him with the lamp! Hurry!" Elle was beside herself. She read his badge. His name was Carl. He was moving in slow motion! "Carl! What are you waiting for? Cuff him!" Elle was shrieking.

The officer bent down and hoisted Agent Carson to a sitting position. Agent Carson felt for his gun. Of course, they were both gone, and he glared at Elle.

She eyed him back. "I took your Glock and your Sig."

"Give me back my weapons." Agent Carson's voice was hoarse and menacing. Carl was finally beginning to question the possibility of danger. He pulled out his cuffs, leaned down, put the agent's hands behind his back, slapped the cuffs on and clicked them shut. Then he helped the agent to a standing position and assisted him to a chair. Carl showed more compassion for the agent than Elle felt at the moment. He went over and got some paper towels to help mop up the blood that had rolled down Carson's neck and soaked into his white shirt collar.

Elle immediately was relieved. She sat down in a chair, exhausted, and felt the tears rising to the surface again. Then she realized the phone was still off the hook. She hurried over and put it back together and returned it to its place on the end table. She left the lamp where it had fallen.

Carl pulled out his notebook. "Just a couple of basic questions for my log, if you don't mind."

More knocking at the door and a loud voice said, "Police!" Carl stayed with the agent while Elle went and let in two uniformed policemen. She opened the door and her face lit up in recognition!

"Hi, you guys! I'm so glad to see you! Oh, uh, in case you don't recognize me, you investigated a break in and a shooting at an office in the Stanford Building.'

Officer Lawson and Officer Armstrong walked into the room and surveyed the situation. Officer Armstrong held out his hand and Elle shook it. He smiled and said, "Miss Wickersham! Hello again!"

Carl was waving at the officers, so Officer Armstrong told Elle to have a seat. He motioned to Officer Lawson to go over and talk to the security guard, so he obliged and sat down with Carl, who right away pointed to Elle explaining she was the complainant. Carl explained what he had witnessed, and Lawson made notes. Then he excused the security guard. In the meantime, Armstrong sat down with Elle so she could tell him her story.

Carl opened the door to leave and there stood George. Carl tipped his cap, exchanged places with George and went off down the hall. Obviously puzzled, George entered the room and shut the door behind him. He immediately saw Elle's tear-stained face.

"Elle? What in the world is going on?" Elle jumped up and burst into tears. He put his arms out and she ran blindly toward him. He caught her and held her while she sobbed. Both officers stood up.

Between sobs, she tried to explain, "Agent Carson came, and he turned out to be not nice, and he said weird things, and then he said he killed Butch, and then he said he might kill me, and he said I shouldn't tell, and then he said he blew up your car, and then he said-- no-- he said he blew up your car first, and then—"

"Wait! What did you just say? Did you say Carson blew up my car?" George looked down into Elle's face. "Is that what you just said? He admitted he blew up my car?" The barely controlled fury was evident in his face and voice.

Through fresh tears and more sobbing Elle nodded. "He said he'd kill me, and then he acted weird-- I mean he acted more weird, and I hit him with a lamp, and I called 911, and I called the desk and asked for security, and yes, he said he blew up your car!" The tears were flowing freely. She put her hands over her face and tried to stop the sobbing. Now, there were tears in George's eyes. He reached for tissues and walked her gently over to the couch and sat her down, still holding her in his arms. He knew this had been brewing for a while. It had been a terrible few days for them both.

He just sat with her and let her cry. He dabbed his own eyes and then Elle's, oblivious for the moment of the two police officers standing there in the room waiting.

Chapter 15

During Elle's meltdown, George made eye contact over Elle's head with Officer Lawson and tried to explain in a nutshell. He explained to them that the stress over the break in at his office, compounded by the murder of Elle's ex, while not knowing who was involved, as well as trying to stay out of sight had taken a toll on both of them. When Elle had finally wound down, George explained he was Elle's friend as well as attorney and asked what they needed him to do. Officer Lawson told him to go ahead and have a seat while his partner attempted to get a statement from the prisoner, with whom he was struggling for cooperation.

Agent Carson had become belligerent, and his voice rose several decibels. Elle was now sure everyone in the hotel heard she made up this wild story and that she tried to seduce him. She was answering questions in her own interview, but it was getting more difficult for her to concentrate and harder for her to be heard over the yelling. She looked over at Agent Carson and gave him a look of disgust.

"Not only are you a criminal, an embarrassment to your country and the FBI, but you are a big fat liar!" She stood up and took a few steps toward him, gingerly reached inside his jacket and pulled out the black book. She stood glaring at him. "This is my personal property, and I'm retrieving it. How could you turn like that? We trusted you!" Then she returned to her place on the couch, ignoring Agent Carson, and faced Officer Armstrong, who opened his mouth to ask a question.

"May I see that?"

Elle's heart did a nervous flip flop. "See what?"

He pointed to the black book. "Is that evidence? Anything to do with why we are here?"

"No," Elle said. "That man is an FBI agent who contacted us after the shooting, the first one, I mean. He apparently came here today pretending to want to discuss the latest information, but it turned out to be a simple case of lechery. He was extremely unprofessional, so I retaliated by kicking him in the shin and stomping on his foot and then I hit him with that lamp."

Officer Armstrong coughed and covered his mouth in a hopeless attempt to keep from laughing out loud. He concentrated intently on his notebook and was somehow able to regain his composure. His partner wasn't as successful. He could hear Lawson snickering, which created more mulishness in his prisoner. Armstrong ran his hand over his blond hair in a futile attempt to focus his attention on the matter at hand.

Now that she'd had her say, Elle sat quietly with George beside her and waited for any other questions. When both officers were finished, Officer Armstrong asked Elle and George to go down to the station and sign their statements. She explained they had to go down there anyway to sign a statement about the blowing up of George's car in the middle of the night. The officer's eyes widened. "Does that have to do with what's going on here?"

George shook his head. "We had thought the car bomb arose from a separate issue. We thought it could have something to do with the shooting and the break in from the other night. But now I'm not so sure. If Carson is telling the truth, I guess he is your man. I do wonder if it's braggadocio. Have you been in touch with Detective Arnold Travis? You probably are going to want to compare notes." Officer Lawson nodded and wrote something in his notebook. Then he told George and Elle he and his partner would take Agent Carson downtown and call his superiors. "Thanks so much for your help. We'll call you if we need anything more. But please don't forget to go down and sign your statements."

Elle gave them a sad smile. "Thank you. We won't forget. Oh, may I have your cards, please. Wait. Never mind. I think I have them from last time."

Officer Lawson smiled. "Here's another one just in case." He handed the card to George and reminded him and Elle to call him any time. George responded with the promise he and Elle were happy to cooperate. She attempted another smile, and the officers took their prisoner and headed for the door.

"Oh! Agent --and I use the term as a joke--Carson!" The men stopped and turned to look at Elle. She looked straight at the agent. "Was it you who tampered with our champagne?"
Agent Carson 's upper lip curled again and then he glared at her. "Don't be ridiculous."

Elle glared back. "So, I'll take that as a yes?"

Agent Carson turned to the officers. "Get me outta here." Officer Armstrong headed down the hall with the agent, but Officer Lawson stayed behind. "Miss Wickersham, do you want to file a complaint about the champagne?"

Elle shook her head and sighed. "Thank you, but I really don't know if it was defective or sabotaged. It's ok. Never mind." The officer touched his hat in an old-fashioned gesture of respect and disappeared.

When everyone had departed, Elle dropped into one of the comfy chairs and sighed. "Is this roller coaster ever going to end?"

George sat down in the other chair with the newspaper. He looked over at Elle. "Soon, I hope. My brain is maxed out. In the meantime, is it time for lunch? My inner clock is broken. After today, more than ever I hate to take you out in public. I don't know where people are and I don't know who's watching, but I feel like you're safer right here – in spite of that stupid Agent Carson's shenanigans. Can we order something?"

Elle yawned. "Fine by me. I'm happy to go nowhere at all."

"What sounds good?" George opened up the hotel information guide.

"What is there?" Elle asked.

"I like this Bethany's Table."

Elle yawned. "Sounds great. Find out if they have soup."

George made the call and asked about soup. He put his hand over the speaker and said, "They have a soup and bread, and the soup of the day is Tomato Basil Parmesan."

"Yes, please."

George put in the order and asked for delivery. He gave them his credit card and where they were staying. He had ordered the BLT for himself and cheesecake with huckleberries for both of them.

When the food arrived, George exercised the same caution as always, only opening the door as much as necessary, and looking up and down the hallway.

The soup was spectacular. Halfway through, Elle actually got up and went to look for her purse. George watched with curiosity. She came back with a small hard cover brown book about the size of a cell phone. She showed the title to him. *My Little Brown Book of Favorite Eating Places.* She opened it up and showed him that the top of each page had a box for the name of the restaurant with the address and the pages were lined like a notebook. Plenty of room to note the highlights of that particular establishment. She explained she had found the book in a souvenir shop some time ago. "It keeps track of all the best places to eat. One page for each place. When you end up at some establishment and the food turns out to be amazing, it gets a page in the book. And look! It fits in my purse!" Elle chuckled. "I don't always remember to write in this book, but this soup is outstanding, and I need to make a note of it!"

They spent the afternoon dozing. George kept one eye on the Mariners game. Elle called her sister, Mandy, to let her know she was all right. George called his sister, Linda, to check in for messages and to make sure she was ok. He told her to work from home for the time being.

George's phone rang. He answered and said, "Oh, Hi Agent Travis!" They talked for a few minutes and Elle was itching to know what Agent Travis was saying since George kept saying, "Oh no." When he was finally off the phone, he looked at Elle and sighed.

"What now? Elle held her breath.

"Your house is trashed."

"Oh no!"

"You cannot go home. They broke the back door. Agent Travis thinks they used a sledgehammer. Every room in the house is damaged. Books out of the bookcases. Drawers pulled out and left on the floor. Closets. Your Mary Engelbreit collection. I don't even want to tell you any more. They slit your mattress open! Butch must have been there. Wouldn't he be the only one that knew the money was between the mattress and box springs?"

Elle stood agape. She put her hand over her mouth and sank onto the sofa. Finally, she said in a small voice, "Don't tell me any more."

She stood up and went over to her bed and pulled the blanket off. She wrapped it around herself and went out onto the balcony and sat in one of the papasan chairs. George came out and sat in the other one. It was warm evening. They sat and watched the sun slide down below the horizon until there was just a sliver left. Elle thought it was cool that their room was situated so they could see both sunrise and sunset and weird that she saw them both in the same day. She wondered if her homeowner's insurance would pay for whatever happened to her house. Maybe she'd have some professional house cleaners come in and clean up the mess. Maybe she'd need a contractor. The she wondered why she was even thinking about stupid stuff like that.

She looked at her watch. It was 7:30. Still a bit light out. She was restless. She stood up and patted George's shoulder and went back in the room. She tossed the blanket on to her bed and paced for a minute and looked at George standing in the doorway. "Are you hungry yet?"

George looked back at her, surprised. He chuckled. "Didn't we just eat? I'm the one that's always hungry, but sure, I could eat. What do you want to do?"

"Let's see if we can find a neighborhood pizza joint, an out of the way place, where no one notices anyone or anything? Could we just sneak out for a while?"

"Dangerous. Why? Why would you want to leave the safety of this hotel room?"

"I've got cabin fever." She sighed and paced back and forth the length of the hotel room. "See? Took me thirty seconds to do that."

George shut his eyes and pinched the bridge of his nose. "Ok. I'll tell you what I think but I won't stop you. If you insist, I will go with you. Whatever happens, I'm not about to let you out of my sight."

They tidied themselves up, locked the hotel room, and headed for the elevators. They stepped out on the main floor and walked through the lobby out onto the sidewalk. Elle breathed in some fresh air. "When this is over, I need a vacation!"

They located the rental car and climbed in. Elle waited until George maneuvered into the flow of traffic and then brought up something she had been thinking about.

"Agent Carson couldn't have killed Butch, could he? Agent Carson. Why am I calling him agent? Well, he was with us at dinner that night and there was no way he could have had time to get there ahead of us. He arrived the same time we did. And we know Butch was still alive then because he attacked me on the way to the restroom."

George scratched his head. "So, if he's bragging about it, then he must have ordered Butch to be killed, which makes me wonder how much power Agent, I mean Mr, I mean that Ass Carson actually has. Is he higher in the food chain than we think?" George shook his head. "It boggles the mind."

Elle watched her side of the street for a not-too-popular eating establishment. "So then who shot Butch? Who is out there doing things to scare us? Why was your office so trashed? What were they looking for? I guess the black book, but how did they know to look there? Who all knows that it was tucked away in your safe? Who have we talked to since then? Have we told anyone? Of course, they've trashed my house, and probably yours and now the offices. What's left?"

George yawned. "Boy, that makes me tired! My head is spinning!"

They ended up in the older part of downtown, just driving around, looking for some hole in the wall.

"Hey, look there, a cute place. It looks Italian. Do you think it's pizza or more upscale?" Elle pointed just up ahead. "Wanna try there?"

George frowned. "I dunno. It looks like they might be shorthanded… See the sign in the window?"
Elle strained to see in the windows. "Hmm. what kind of a sign is that? 'Special Help Wanted.' What's the name of this place?"

George read the sign. "Berlusconi."
Suddenly, Elle was famished. "Well, that's a good Italian name! Let's try it!"

When they walked in, Elle's mouth fell open. This was no Pizza joint. Berlusconi was everything Elle ever imagined an Italian restaurant should be. Polished dark wood, heavy brocade drapes, overstuffed chairs, displays of wine everywhere. It almost seemed like someone's home rather than a restaurant. There was an old-fashioned pool table down at one end, and the bar was low with overstuffed chairs for seating there as well. Healthy plants decorated the tables scattered throughout. More greenery cascaded from wall sconces. Mixed smells of garlic and baking bread wafted their way through the air and floated past Elle's nose waking up those hunger pangs.

They chose to be shown to a table right away rather than sit at the bar. Their server introduced himself as Aldo, which, he was proud to say, meant "old and wise." He spoke enough English that they were able to communicate easily. Thankfully the menu was in English. They took their time. Aldo brought a bottle of wine, his recommendation. Then came a basket of Focaccia bread with a veritable smorgasbord of toppings: Herbs and garlic, olives, tomatoes, sesame seeds, parmesan cheese, pine nuts, pesto, caramelized onions, and more.

"So much for my great plans this morning," Elle mumbled. "What great plans?" George lowered his menu so he could see her face.

"Oh, just to make sure I can still squeeze my body into my uniform." She rolled her eyes.

"We'll start tomorrow," George assured her.

She smirked. "You know tomorrow never comes?"

Aldo saved George from thinking up a response. Aldo invited them to try a 'delizioso!' "It's an Italian martini made with lively Italian flavors, including Campari, honey, lemon and fresh basil!"

George said, "Why not? Let's eat, drink, and be merry for tomorrow we shall diet!"

Elle rolled her eyes.

Aldo was back almost immediately with the drinks. He stood anxiously while they did the taste test and he smiled broadly when George gave him the thumbs up and said the drinks were awesome! Then Aldo asked them if they were ready to order.

It was a difficult decision, but Elle finally chose the Cheese Ravioletti in Pink Sauce. She read the description to George. "Cheese-stuffed Ravioletti smothered with a thick, zesty sauce made from white wine, pureed tomatoes and rich cream." He agreed it sounded delizioso!

George's choice was Chicken with Mustard Mascarpone Marsala Sauce. He read the description to Elle: "Chicken breasts smothered in a Marsala wine cream sauce with mushrooms and served with tender fettuccine. She agreed it sounded 'delizioso!

Once the ordering was complete, they sat and admired the scenery.

Elle sighed. "I can't believe I can enjoy food knowing that someone is out to kill us. And I still can't believe Agent—I mean that guy Carson-- has turned out to be a criminal. Well, not so much a criminal, but also a lech! You can't believe how he stepped over the line of decency with me!"

George sat up straight. "Did he hurt you? Touch you inappropriately? I'll wring his neck!"

Elle put her hands out across the table and held his. "Please, George, believe me. He did not touch me. He got close, but it was all lecherous talk. And I can't believe I kicked him in the shin! And then stomped on his foot! I've never hit or hurt a man in my life! I wasn't even thinking about his gun!"

George was smiling. He was relaxed again. "I'm so sorry I missed it! But it's really good to know that when push comes to shove, or kick versus stomp, pardon my pun, you can take care of yourself! That's really comforting for me, and knowing your past, I don't know why I was even worried!"

Elle assured him. "I mean, now that I've grown up, I don't ever kick or stomp on people. Believe me, it was pure reflex! I was really mad!"

George frowned. "I feel duped. Agent Carson was really great in the beginning! Maybe he's schizophrenic? I mean, how could he be so professional and compassionate and then turn out to be a whack job?"

Elle smirked. "You're just like my dad. When he can't figure out why someone is behaving so stupidly, he says they have a brain tumor."

George agreed. "Well? That's almost like schizophrenia, right? Something is amuck in the brain box."

Their food arrived and they made inroads. The food was good. Elle took a few bites and put her fork down.

"George, I'm sorry I made you come out tonight. I think I should be in mourning. Shouldn't I? Why am I out having some really great food when Butch is dead? I should be dressing in black and eating bread and water. Well, maybe not bread and water, but do you think I'm callous? Should I be sad?"

George put his fork down too. "Elle, you can't help what you feel. You can't pretend to mourn someone who treated you so badly. You don't need to dance on the table, but there is no point in putting on sackcloth and ashes for someone who tortured you. Am I making sense? You have every right to be relieved an unhappy chapter in your life is now over."

Elle sat for a moment absorbing George's wisdom. She gave a great sigh, something she'd been doing quite a lot lately. "Thanks George."

Elle felt better. Still not sure what to think about Butch, but she now realized she couldn't change the past. It was finished. They both turned their attention to their plates.

Aldo brought cappuccinos for both of them along with the bill.

Elle sighed. "I'm so full. I'm not sure I can walk. Just roll me out to the car."

George agreed. He yawned. "We need sleep now."

She sat back in her comfortable chair. "Are you paying, or am I?"

"I'm getting this. Do you have any cash left? Do you want to leave the tip?"

George tucked his credit card in the pocket of the leather folder.

"Sure." She rummaged around in her purse and felt the black book. She set it on the table and went back in for more cash. She laid some bills down and picked up the book and glanced at the inside cover.

"George!" she said too loudly. She sat up straight in her chair. "Listen to this!"

George, mouthful of cappuccino, jumped, swallowed, choked and coughed.

Elle frowned and waited. "Do I need to pat you on the back or call a medic?"

George wiped his eyes and took a sip of water. "Thanks for not calling attention to us. I'm pretty sure I'll live. No need for a medic."

Elle felt bad. "I'm really sorry. I didn't mean to startle you."

George grinned. "Well, you certainly got my attention!" She looked around to see if anyone was listening. They were the only ones left in the dining room. She lowered her voice. "Listen to this: 13744 SW Lakeview Avenue. Sign in the window Special Help Wanted. Paper Towel. What does that mean? Aren't we on Lakeview Avenue?"

George sat still, his mind whirling.

Elle started to say something, but he held up his hand.

"We need to leave right now. Quietly. With as little fuss as possible. Don't look. I just saw Mutt and Jeff disappear down the hall."

Chapter 16

George picked up the folder with his credit card in it, and hearts pounding, they very calmly and quietly got up and began walking toward the entrance. Elle could feel sweat droplets on the back of her neck under her hair. Aldo caught up with them and George handed him the folder. They stood, striving to look calm, while the business was transacted. George signed the restaurant copy and grabbed his. Aldo thanked them for coming in. They smiled stiffly and ducked out.

Forcing themselves to at least look calm, hardly breathing, they walked to the car. When they were close, they both leapt into the rental. The doors were barely closed, and George stepped on the gas. He drove as fast as he dared, keeping an eye on his rear-view mirror. Several miles later, when he had decided they weren't being followed, he steered into a Safeway parking lot. He picked an area heavily populated with cars, pulled in to an empty spot and turned off the engine. They both heaved a sigh of relief. Elle was still sweating. She asked George to turn the key so she could roll down her window. The night air moved across her face, and she leaned back and closed her eyes. They sat there quietly for a few minutes, waiting for their blood pressures to return to normal range.

In a very small voice, Elle said, "I can't believe out of all the eating establishments in Portland we chose that one."

George staring straight ahead, cleared his throat. "Talk about your irony. Whew! I think we should get back to the hotel ASAP, don't you?" He started the car. "Let's go."

They headed straight for their hotel. When they arrived, they parked in a populated area with other cars, locked up and made a beeline for their room.

George locked the door and sat down on the end of the closest bed, wearily kicking off his shoes. He yawned. He looked over at Elle, who was slumped in one of the overstuffed chairs, eyes closed.

He went over and helped Elle up and walked her over to the bed. He pulled back the bed spread, blanket, and sheet and sat her down. He removed her flip flops and then he picked her up in his arms, gently laid her down, and pulled the covers up to her chin. He kissed her on the forehead. And then he sprawled out on the other bed. He was out before his head hit the pillow.

~~~#~~~

The Sunday morning sun streamed into the room filling every nook and cranny with warmth. Elle opened her eyes and wondered how she ended up in bed, once again, with all her clothes on. She looked over at George. He was wrapped up like a cocoon in the bedspread on the other bed. Memories of yesterday floated to the surface of her mind and she decided she'd just stay right where she was for the rest of her life.

George sat up. "Elle?" He whispered.

"I'm awake. Thanks for not leaving me sitting in that chair all night."

"At your service, mademoiselle! How about some breakfast? I'm starving!"

"After all that food we ate last night?" Elle groaned. She pushed away her covers and sighed. It would be nice to wear pajamas again one of these nights. She was tired of sleeping in her clothes. In fact, she was tired of being a nomad. She scooted up to a sitting position against the pillows and waited for George to order breakfast.

George rolled off his bed and stood up. "I'm calling room service. What do you want? Bagel? Caramel Macchiato?"

Elle chuckled. "Obviously I'm in a serious rut. Yes. Bagel, cream cheese, just regular black coffee with creamer. Ask them if they have flavored creamer, please?"

George picked up the phone and dialed room service.

"Hi I'd like to order a bagel, cream cheese, black coffee. Do you have flavored creamer? Yes? What kind please? Vanilla caramel will be fine. Also, an order of pancakes, extra syrup, sausage, scrambled eggs, do you have Heinz 57? Good. And another coffee. Thank you."

Elle pulled the sheet up over her knees to get cozier. "I need to do some laundry or something. I need clean clothes. What are we going to do today?"

"I think you need to stay out of sight. I hope we didn't shoot ourselves in the foot last night. We need to do something about Butch's car. We need to get that black book to the authorities. FBI? Or police? In fact…" George used his cell phone to call Jack. "Hey, it's George. Is there someone somewhere in law enforcement that you like and trust? We really need to talk to someone. We just don't know who." George listened for a few minutes, said his thanks, then hung up.

"There is a guy he went to police academy with that he trusts with his life. You won't believe who it is. He was a police detective, but he moved over to the FBI so now he's Agent Arnie Travis. How do you like that? After finding out about Agent Carson, I was ready to think the whole police force and the whole FBI are criminals. You have his card, don't you? I think we should call him."

Locating her purse Elle extricated Detective Travis' card. "Would his number be the same?" Elle asked. "I mean, don't they get their phones provided by the department? So, if he changed jobs, he'd have a new cell phone, right?"

George punched the buttons on the phone. "I think this is his personal cell number. We'll see."

"Yes, hello, I'm looking for Detective Arnie Travis, I mean Agent Arnie Travis. Oh, good. This is George Wendling. You investigated a murder at my office on Wednesday night. Yes, the murder of Butch Kennedy. We'd like to come see you or meet you somewhere so we could talk if that is possible. Yes, I like that idea. Great! Thanks so much! See you later!" He put his phone back in his pocket.

"We are going to meet him at the bowling alley in the Wilson Street Shopping Center. It's really busy so we'll just get lost in the crowd. He's off at 3 p.m. so we'll see him about 3:30."

Knocking at the door put George in caution mode. As always, he opened the door just a crack to see who it was. There was the waiter from room service. As was the usual routine, he told them to put the tray on the floor. He brought it in after they had gone into the elevator.

George ate with gusto. Elle drank her coffee. She bit off a piece of bagel and chewed. "You're going to have to find me a suitcase for all these clothes. Maybe stop at Goodwill? See if you can find an inexpensive carry-all or something? If you get me something at Goodwill it wouldn't be such a strain on your wallet, or I could just give you my credit card."

George's heart did a Michael Jackson moon walk. Just one of the many things he loved about her. She was never a snob about money. The whole world was her shopping mall. She wasn't the least bit ashamed or embarrassed to shop at Goodwill. In fact, they loved to go in there to see what was new. It was always a surprise to find items that were fascinating to them. They could never figure out how one man's trash was another man's treasure. Elle could find cute clothes anywhere. Oh, he knew she loved cute clothing from expensive boutiques, but she was sensible. She had never been interested in just throwing her money away. She had never cared about labels.

When he was finished with his breakfast, he washed his hands at the kitchen sink. He grabbed his jacket while admonishing Elle not to open the door to anyone.

She told him to be careful, and he was out the door. She sat for a while longer finishing her coffee ticking things off her list in her head. First on the list was to call work. She picked up the phone and pressed buttons. "Scheduling, please." She hummed along with the hold music. "Yes. Hi! This is Elle Wickersham. I need to skip my next flight please. I have a family emergency. Yes. Actually, I need to request two weeks at this point. Thanks. Ok. That will be fine. Thank you. Oh, how much vacation time do I have left? Ok. Great! Thank you. Sorry, what? Oh! Yes, I'll tell my supervisor. For sure. Thanks."

She ended that call then pressed buttons, listening for a response. "Betsy, oh good. Glad I caught you. It's Elle. I just talked to scheduling. I requested two weeks leave, but I wanted to let you know… What? What? When? O my gosh! What did these guys look like? Really? You didn't tell them anything did you? Oh. Good. Don't. It's a long story, but I'll tell you all about it when it's over. Just don't tell anyone anything about me. Thanks!"

She sat on the edge of the bed, wishing George would get back soon and wondering what else was around the corner.

George returned to the hotel room, refreshed, dressed in gray slacks, black dress shirt, and black and gray striped tie slung around his neck. His belt and shoes were black. Elle loved how he cared about how he looked. His hair was still damp, and his face was still reddened, and it was nearly noon. Those were the clues that told her he had taken the time to do his run before showering and dressing. He showed Elle what he had brought for her today. Black jeans, black T-shirt with a heart of silver sparkles on the front, and red sweatshirt that said "Oregon." And a huge red canvas shoulder tote with sparkles on the front.

Elle's eyes widened, first at how good George looked. "You look really good!" She glowed when she observed everything he had brought. "You're the man! I can't believe you found this! You have out done yourself! I love it all!"

"Well... I got a little spooked when I started toward home. So I went to Linda's and showered and changed there. These are Stewie's clothes. Nice, huh?"

Elle smiled. "Good thing you and your brother-in-law are the same size! You look really good!"

George reddened slightly. "Good! Now go get ready. I'm starving, so I'm ordering lunch. What do you want?"

"See if there is a taco salad and get it with chicken if they have it please," she called from the bathroom. "No shell, please. I'm not going to fit into my uniform!"

"Oh! Did you talk to someone at your work?"

"Yeah, I was going to tell you. I took two weeks off. This has got to be all over by then, or I think I might shoot someone. Yikes! That was a poor choice of words. Ugh. I can't believe I said that." She went into the bathroom and shut the door.

The door immediately flew back open and Elle came out of the bathroom. "Butch was a big blabbermouth! He told those idiots where I work! He actually went there with those two goons and talked to Betsy! As if she'd know where I'm when I'm off duty. Why couldn't he have just kept me out of it? Stupid man. I keep thinking I've seen the worst and even now, I learn things I don't want to know about him! Gahh!"

George heard the shower start while he was calling room service. While Elle dressed, he sat down in one of the overstuffed chairs by the window in the living room area. He loved the view of the Willamette River. Then he swiveled to do a pan of the hotel suite. He eyed the room critically. It was decorated in pale blue and beige. The carpet was a darker blue which matched the throw pillows on the beds. It was a good arrangement. The beds were close to the entrance, a good thing it seemed lately. Beyond the beds was the living area with four comfy chairs. The kitchenette was against the wall to the left with the round table close by. He was really getting to like living here. Well, he was honest enough to admit being with Elle was heaven-- hence he really didn't care where he was as long as she was with him. This room will have precious memories for me, he thought.

The food arrived and Elle appeared all dressed, hair still damp. They sat at the round table side by side eating their lunch.

"Elle," George put his hand over hers. "Are you over him? Do you still love him?"

Elle looked into his face. She wanted him to know the truth. "George. I'll tell you the truth. He wore me out. He was higher maintenance than six models prepped for the runway. Self-preservation was his number one priority. Selfishness oozed out of him like toxic leakage. He sucked everything out of me and there were days when I was sure all his chairs weren't under the table. He said weird things to me. He was high or drunk most of the time. Or it was his alter ego, or one of his other personalities. This last year I've felt nothing. Just exhaustion. And then that day he said those words to me…"

Elle's mouth was open, but nothing came out. "I can't even say them to you. They're words I'll never forget and if there were any feelings left in me, those dried up and blew away that Wednesday night. I was angry and hurt, but if I could admit it, I felt free. I felt guilty for not feeling guilty. Oh, those words hurt. But they woke me up. I was done. I am done. Butch is a bad dream in my past." She looked lovingly at George. "You don't have to worry about that. There is no torch. Never will be."

George looked closer into her eyes.

She squinted. "What's with the x-ray vision?"

"Just making sure you're telling the truth."

"I'm telling the truth. Have I ever lied to you?"

"Yes. When we were nine, you told me I was adopted."

Elle burst out laughing!

George sniffed. "It took a long time to get over that." He dramatically put his hand to his forehead and sighed.

Elle was still laughing. "I did apologize, didn't I?"

"Yes, but I could be scarred for life!"

Elle's heart gave a lurch. She tried to keep it light. "Am I going to have to do penance for that?"

"Yes." He leaned closer. "I'm going to have to gravely ponder this issue."

She moved her face closer. "And?" Another inch and her lips were on his. Then she jumped back startled. They stared at each other in shock. His arm reached out and pulled her chair towards him. And then he was kissing her.

She pushed him away and took a breath. "Wow! And I've been avoiding that all this time!"

He grinned, determined to keep it light. "Yup. It's all your own fault!"

He leaned into her and kissed her again. Then he hopped up and said, "I'd very much like to just kiss you all day, but we have an appointment. OH! I almost forgot! Your dad called me. Linda has been keeping them posted, but he was worried you might need some money. He actually gave Linda a check for $5000 made out to me because he figured I was helping you."

Elle's eyes filled with tears. "That is so my dad. I can't imagine what he's going through! I'll call him tonight and thank him. Thank God for Linda! I haven't wanted to talk to my parents because I'd cry and then they would worry more. I haven't been keeping track, but is $5000 going to be enough?"

George smiled. "It's plenty."

They stared at each other, both feeling weird and warm and fuzzy. Elle felt a niggling of guilt. This was absolutely not how it was supposed to be. George was strictly off limits!

Chapter 17

"OK! Back to business!" George grabbed the key card off the table. "Is this mine or yours? Well, it's in my pocket." He headed to the door. "Are you coming?"

Elle was still in her chair, feeling that kiss.   Mixed emotions flooded her brain. What just happened? Whatever possessed her to do that? She shouldn't have done that! What about her code??? Must not fall in love with George! Then she chuckled to herself. But that was so nice. And then... $5000! My life is so weird right now, but I need to be more careful. I don't want George to get the wrong idea!

She followed George out of the room and shut the door. She caught up with him and they got in the elevator together.   On the main floor, they walked across the lobby to the front doors and out into the sunshine. Keeping their eyes open for anything unusual, they got in the rental and George pointed the nose of the car out into the busy traffic.

They parked the car in a heavily populated area and entered the bowling alley. Agent Travis was sitting in a corner of the restaurant drinking a soda. They joined him, and Agent Travis signaled the server. She came over to see what they wanted. George ordered a beer, and Elle asked for a Bloody Mary.

"So," Agent Travis sat forward with his elbows on the table. "What's this all about?"

George looked at the agent's soda. "You're not drinking?"

Agent Travis chuckled. "I'm not really ready to start drinking this early. I'm taking my wife out for dinner tonight, so I need to be alert."

Elle and George both smiled.

George explained about the black book, and they told him everything they could think of, including last night in the restaurant and the incident with Agent Carson. Elle looked around and didn't see anyone paying any attention, so she slipped him the book. He looked at the inside cover.

"What do you think 'paper towel' means?" Elle asked, "Is it maybe a code or something?"

George chuckled. "It's probably his grocery list."

All three of them laughed.

Agent Travis replied, "It could be some kind of message. Tell me about this place where you were."

They both went into more detail, but neither of them had taken a look around to see what else was on the premises.

"When we saw Mutt and Jeff, we just wanted to get out of there." George grimaced. "We should have gone to the restroom so we could see more of the back rooms… restroom… paper towel… could it be as simple as that? Something to do with paper towels?"

Agent Travis looked puzzled. "Mutt and Jeff?"

"Oh," George chuckled. "That's Elle's way of describing the two goons who came to my office the other night. One was tall and the other one short, and they were wearing retro clothes like from the 1920's. The shrimpy guy seemed to be calling the shots so that's why he got to be Jeff.

Agent Travis smiled. "I've a good idea who they were! It sounds like Tony Romano and Franco Rossi. They're a couple of lackeys for hire. They mostly work for a crime boss named Alonzo Bianci. Alonzo isn't the top dog, but he is more visible than the boss. We haven't been able to discover who the really big boss is.

George snapped his fingers. "That's it! We heard one of them call the other one Tony!"

Elle perked up. "Yes! I'm sure they had no idea we were paying that much attention to what they were saying. And about the other thing. Well, it would have to be kind of simple. We're dealing with Butch after all, and he was no Mensa candidate. Sorry. I shouldn't speak ill of the dead." She took a deep breath. "Agent

Travis, I've a small list of requests and I was wondering if you have jurisdiction over these particular items. I don't want to ask you to do something not in your job description, nor am I trying to tell you how to do your job."

Agent Travis looked benignly at her. "Please ask me what you want to. I'll say 'yes' if I can and 'no' if I can't. Is that fair?"

Elle was pleased. "Yes, that's more than fair! So, first of all, I wonder if maybe you should check George's house. If mine is in bad shape, I'm worried about his. Could someone take care of that?"

Agent Travis nodded. I agree. I have some men on the way over there now. I've been worried about his house since we discovered the battering your house took. Another question for me?"

"Actually, you have already answered the first question. I was kind of tired of calling them Mutt and Jeff for much longer. So, is there any way you can make sure it's those two little criminals?"

The agent thought a minute. "I think we may have gotten some DNA from those bozos so it may be possible. Next question?"

Elle looked at her list. "Oh, is there someone who could check on Gus, the Pastry Guru? He was in the office that day Mutt and Jeff burst in and they may have gotten a good look at him. I'm worried about his safety, although he is on the go most of the day with deliveries so he might be safe enough, but I'd feel better if someone could look in on him."

Agent Travis nodded. "I think we can take care of that." Elle consulted her list again. "Just one more thing. Butch's car is somewhere. We don't know where. You may want to search it for any clues that might help us find Mr. Big or whoever is behind all this. Can you put out an APB? Or BOLO?"

Agent Travis smiled at her use of police jargon. "Yes, we can do that. Do you know where it was last seen?"

George spoke up. "It could be in the parking garage in my building, the Stanford Building. It's a blue Camaro, License SEXY1."

"OK, I'll put the word out and have some boys go take a look. We'll impound it and search it. In the meantime, Elle, you probably shouldn't go home. As I told George, it's a mess. And forensics has been there and so there's black dust everywhere."

Elle chuckled. "Well, that will go nicely with all the brown dust!" She felt a whole lot better. "Yes, I agree. I'd like to know who has been there. Do we get to see the photos?"

The agent hesitated. "I'll check on that. I'm not in favor of sharing information on an open investigation and it's against the rules. I'll have to think about that. No promises, ok?"

"Thanks, Agent Travis, that's more than fair. We really appreciate it. After dealing with Agent Carson, we were kind of at a loss for someone to trust in law enforcement."

Agent Travis stood up and threw a five-dollar bill on the table. "No worries. We've had our eye on Carson for some time. His behavior has just not been totally kosher lately. I can't put my finger on it, but I really think he's mixed up in something unsavory. We just can't nail him down. We haven't said anything to him because we don't want to spook him. But he's being watched all the time."

George grabbed the five and handed it back. "We've got this," he said. "Oh, wait, is it ok for me to pick up the tab? It's not unethical for you, is it?"

Agent Travis smiled. "No, it's fine. Here's the rule: 'A gift does not include items such as modest items of food and non-alcoholic refreshments, such as soft drinks, coffee and donuts, offered other than as part of a meal.'"

Elle and George both thanked him for seeing them and for helping them, and the agent left to go meet his dinner date.

George paid the bill while Elle waited for him. They walked out of the restaurant and casually looked around. It seemed clear, so they forced themselves to stroll through the bowling alley towards the door, in spite of their nerves twitching. George kept his eyes busy roving back and forth checking for any movement that might be suspicious.

"Elle?"

"Yes?"

"Butch's new car was a blue Camaro."

"Right."

"License plate SEXY1."

"Yes. Why are you saying that?"

"It's driving around the parking lot."

They stood on the sidewalk wondering whether to head to the car or go back inside the building. George was frantically searching for the vehicle.

"So where is it now?" Elle was trying not to panic.

"I can't see it right this minute."

"Let's go back inside the lobby and wait for a few minutes." Elle turned around and stopped. "I've got something in my shoe." She grabbed hold of George to steady herself while she kicked off her flip flop and extricated a pebble stuck to the bottom of her bare foot. A bee buzzed by in front of her and she let go of George and stepped back. Suddenly George was on the cement in front of her.

"George! What are you doing?"

"I think I've been shot!" he was panting.

Chapter 18

"I thought it was a bee, but it was a bullet!" Elle burst into tears and dropped to her knees. "Oh No! Why? Where are you hurt? What is happening?" She dug in her purse for her phone and called 911. She held the phone with her right hand and bent over George and put her left arm around his head. Trying not to cry she explained the nature of the emergency -- a bullet wound and the need for an ambulance tout suite!

George had his hand on his right thigh, but the blood was turning his jeans red, seeping through his fingers and making a puddle on the sidewalk. A crowd had begun to gather. Someone had the sense to run for some towels, which were delivered through the sea of gawking bodies by a sympathetic young man who said he was an off-duty paramedic. He put the towels on George's thigh and pushed down hard and held them. In a moment they heard the sirens.

Elle looked down at George. He was sweating and pale. "You're going to be ok, my darling, really. Can you hear the sirens?" He attempted a smile, failed, and whispered a faint thank you. He shut his eyes. A multitude of vehicles began to arrive, lights flashing, sirens blaring.

The paramedics appeared and took over. Elle, still on her knees, weeping, watched George's face anxiously. They got him hooked up to an IV, did vitals, and got him tucked up on the stretcher and loaded him into the ambulance.

A police officer materialized beside Elle while the paramedics were working on George. Elle stood up.

He showed her his ID and identified himself. "Hi, I'm Dillon McCarty. Are you next of kin?"

Elle nodded. "I'm as close as next of kin right now."

The officer had his notebook out. "Just a bit of information, please. I know you want to go with your friend in the ambulance, so I won't keep you. Just his name and yours and then I can meet you at the hospital for a full report. Will that be ok?"

Elle wiped her eyes. "Yes," she said. "That would be fine." She gave the officer her name, address, phone number and George's information too. Then the officer walked her over to where George was being lifted into the ambulance, and after George was settled, Officer McCarty helped her up into the vehicle.

The doors were closed, followed by that double slap on the side, the well-known code for "all clear" and they were off on the fastest ride Elle had ever had. Elle held George's hand and every now and then gave it a squeeze in hopes of a return squeeze. He was obviously too weak from loss of blood.

Their approach to the emergency room brought people running out to help. As they whisked the stretcher away, they were met by the surgical team who ran with them down the hall and out of sight. Elle stood trying to have a complete thought. She walked over to the desk and said, "I'm here with George Wendling. They just took him somewhere, possibly to surgery."

The lady at the desk smiled sympathetically at her and asked her if she could help with information. Elle nodded as she was handed a clip board. She sat and answered as many questions as she could – which was just about all of them—and returned the clip board to the desk.

She asked the receptionist if there was any news and where George actually was. The receptionist looking at her computer informed her he was in the main OR and she could go down that same hall and over to the main elevators and follow the signs to the surgery waiting area. Elle thanked her and the lady said, 'My dear, your young man is in the best of hands." New tears rolled down her cheeks and she smiled tearfully and thanked the lady.

She followed the directions and arrived in the surgery waiting area. She stopped at the information desk and asked if there was any news. This lady was wearing a turquoise volunteer jacket. Her name tag said "Florence." She checked her book and asked for George's name. Elle told her. Florence wrote a number on a sticky note and handed it to her. She told her this was George's code number, and she could watch the progress on the monitor on the wall. Florence pointed to a TV hanging in the corner of the waiting room. She told Elle he was still in the operating room and Dr Bennett would come here to the waiting room to give a report. She showed Elle how to follow the code number from Operating Room to Recovery. Elle thanked her and went to sit down. She stood up again, realizing she should call Linda. She went out in the hall to make her phone call.

"Oh, no! Is he ok? Is he -is he alive?" Linda was understandably shocked.

Elle assured her he was in the best of hands. "We're at OHSU. I'm in the Main OR surgery waiting room. He is in surgery right now and I'm just waiting for some further word."

"OK. I'm on my way!" Linda said tearfully and hung up.

Elle sat down again in the waiting area and wondered if she should call her sister. It had been a while since they had talked. Her sister could not stand the sight of Butch and she had tried for many years to get Elle to dump him. "Well, sis, you got your wish" she said softly.

Just then, Officer McCarty walked in. He stopped at Florence's desk and asked her a question. She nodded. He thanked her. Then he looked around the room, spotted Elle and went over and sat down beside her.

"How are you holding up?" He smiled at her.

"Oh, you know. The best I can," Elle smiled her lopsided smile.

"Would you like to move over into this glass interview room so we can have some privacy?" He pointed to a glass cubicle behind Florence's desk. "I checked with the lady at the desk, and she said it's free right now."

Elle nodded and they both stood up. She followed him over to the glass office and they sat down at the table. He had his notebook out. She recited everything that happened, trying to tell it sequentially. He made notes. She explained about spotting Butch's car and Butch was dead and he had been killed in George's office. She looked in her wallet and took out the cards from the other officers and gave Officer McCarty their names so he could put them in the loop. The tears flowed, and once, the officer left the room to get some tissues from Florence.

When she had told him everything she could remember, the officer closed his notebook and told her he'd have the notes transcribed and asked her to go down to the station and sign the statement. Elle sighed. That was, unfortunately, becoming a familiar request.

After Officer McCarty left, Elle went back out into the hallway to call her sister. When Mandy answered it sounded like she was in the car. Probably on her way home from work. Elle had no idea what time it was. Time had no meaning for her at this moment. Mandy was glad to hear from her. Poor sis, she had no idea what Elle was about to lay on her. She decided not to tell her every detail right now. She'd fill her in later. She told her she was at OHSU with George, and he'd been shot in the thigh. Mandy said she was turning around, and she'd be on her way back to the hospital.

Elle hadn't even tried to call Mandy's office. She hadn't been thinking straight and had no clue even what day it was. Her sister was an employee at OHSU. Actually, she was the executive assistant to the director of Graduate Medical Education. Something to do with new doctors arriving to do their internships.

Elle sat back down again. Her phone beeped. It was a text from Linda. "Where are you?" She texted back some directions from the parking garage. Right away she got another text from Mandy asking where she was. She texted back Main OR surgery waiting room. Mandy knew her way around the hospital.

Elle didn't feel like reading. She didn't feel like looking at her phone. So, she just sat with her eyes closed, willing George to live.

Mandy and Linda arrived together. There were hugs all around before they sat down. Elle brought them up to date.

"Miss Wickersham?" Florence called out her name. Elle jumped up. "What's happening? Where is George?"

Florence took her out in the hallway where Dr Bennett was waiting for her. Elle's heart was doing flip flops. "Is he... Is he alive?"

The surgeon seemed satisfied. "Yes! He did very well! I shouldn't be telling this to you. You're not officially related to him, are you?"

Elle said, "Wait. His sister is here. I'll get her." She rushed back into the room and grabbed Linda's hand. "Dr Bennett wants to tell you about George"

Linda pulled back. "Oh, Elle, I'm frightened. I don't do well with sick kids and brothers." The tears were rolling. Elle put her arm around Linda. "It will be ok. I'll go with you." Linda sighed. "Stewart was the one who always handled the sick stuff. I was worthless!"

Elle smiled sympathetically. Linda's husband was a trooper. She chuckled to herself at the pun she just created. Stewart was not only strong and could handle anything, but he also really was a trooper! A State Trooper. But right now, she was desperate to know something so she gently but firmly propelled Linda out into the hall.

They stood with the surgeon and Elle felt the tears starting to flow again. "Could you just tell us if he's going to live?" The surgeon sighed and smiled wearily. "The bullet nicked the artery, so he lost a lot of blood. We had to transfuse him, but he did well during the procedure and he's on his way to recovery."

Tears rolling down her cheeks, still holding on to Linda, also crying, Elle shook his hand. "I can't tell you how much I appreciate everything you've done. We really would like to see him. Is that possible?"

"Well," Dr Bennett hesitated. "Normally, we don't allow visitors in stage one, but there is only one other patient in there, so I'll give you a few minutes." He walked them into recovery and motioned to one of the nurses to come over. "Give these young ladies just a few minutes, please?"

"Yes, doctor." She led the girls over to George and pulled up chairs for them. Elle let Linda sit closest. She sat and rested her arms on the edge of the bed by his face and put her head down. Linda whispered into his ear that she loved him and to hurry up and get well.

Then she turned to Elle. "I need air. I'm going out in the hall, ok?"

One look at Linda's face which was a shade of white, Elle hugged her and said she'd be there in a minute. "I'll meet you back in the waiting room, ok?" Linda nodded and tiptoed out.

Elle sat down in the chair that Linda had just vacated. The tears came afresh, and she wept silently. "Oh, George," she whispered, "I'm so sorry. It's all my fault. If I'd left Butch when I first had the chance this never would have happened! Why, oh why, did I stay so long? It should have been me that got shot. How can you ever forgive me? Oh, George, please live. I need you. I love you so much!"

She sat up to blow her nose and wipe her face. She leaned closer to examine George's face. His lips were moving slightly. She leaned even closer, and she heard the words, "I love you, Elle."

She reached for his hand and held it until the nurse came to shoo her out. She asked the nurse what would happen next, and she was told George would stay in recovery until he was stable and then be taken upstairs to his room. He'd probably sleep for a while. Elle walked with the nurse out of recovery and into the hallway. "Do you know what room George is going to be in?"

"Let me get his chart and take a look." The nurse disappeared into the recovery area. In a minute she was back. "He will be on 6 North, room 601."

Elle thanked her and hurried down the hall to the elevators. She hopped into the first one that opened and touched number 6. When she arrived on the floor, she walked down to the 6 North nursing station and looked for the ward secretary. She spotted her with a cup of coffee in her hand just sitting down at her desk. Elle went and stood in front of the secretary.

The secretary said, "Hi, may I help you?" Elle identified herself. "I'm here in the hospital with George Wendling. He's in post op right now, but I understand he will be here on this floor in room 601. Is that correct?"

The secretary looked at her notes and told her that was true. Elle told her she was the one that had filled out all the paperwork and it was her number that was the contact number. "I was wondering if you could call me if I'm not here when he wakes up."

The secretary nodded. "I'll let his nurse know." "Thank you so much. I'll be back. I'm just going to go and get some food."

Elle hurried down the hall to the elevator and was back down on the lower level in the surgery waiting room in a few minutes. Mandy and Linda were there and it looked like Mandy was comforting Linda and trying to help her calm down.

Elle asked them if they wanted to go have a cup of coffee. Linda looked at Elle. "I don't know. My stomach is a bit queasy. I feel strange, like I need a good cry."

Mandy and Elle both put their arms around Linda. Mandy said, "I'm so sorry. This is hard on you too! It's your baby brother in there!"

Mandy turned to Elle. "How about if we just go up to the third floor and get some soup or something. Let's go to the Marquam Cafe because it's open 24 hours, and they have the most choices. A lot of the other spots around the hospital complex are mostly coffee and pastries."

Elle agreed. "Marquam is ok by me. And it's a good thing there are many espresso bars!" Elle commented. "Think about it! There would have to be since there are a million beds in this hospital. Even if only one person was visiting each patient that would be over a million people needing coffee, not to mention all the employees! It boggles the mind!"

Mandy rolled her eyes. "Actually, we have 576 beds. You might have exaggerated, just slightly."

Elle looked meekly at her. "Sorry. Can't help it."

Mandy looked at Linda. "OK with you, Lin, if we just get soup upstairs?"

Linda nodded. "I'm in. Let's go there."

After Elle let Florence know where they were going, the three girls walked to the elevators and waited for one going up. The first one that slid open was nearly full, so they waited for another one. The next one had a bit more room, so they got on and rode to the third floor.

They walked around the café looking at all the options. Linda found some soup that sounded good. Elle was feeling a little queasy herself. She knew she was probably hungry. She hadn't eaten since noon and that was hours ago! She decided she'd have a sandwich. She stood at the sandwich bar waiting her turn when she saw on the menu she could have turkey, cream cheese and cranberry sauce. One of her favorite combinations. She put in her order. While she was waiting, she poured herself some fresh hot coffee and grabbed a couple of creamers. Mandy chose coffee and a sandwich too. They went through the line to pay and met up at a table.

Mandy put her hand on her sister's arm. "Elle, talk to me. What is going on?"

Elle looked over at Linda. "Well, first of all, Lin, are you feeling somewhat better?"

Linda smiled and nodded. "This soup is just what I needed! I don't remember eating lunch!"

Elle told the girls how they had gone to the bowling alley to meet the FBI agent. The bowling alley was a really busy place so they were hoping they could hide in the crowd unnoticed. Then George got shot.

Mandy stopped her. "But how did all this happen? How ever did you get mixed up with the FBI? Why did George get shot?"

Elle responded sadly. "It's my fault. If I'd left Butch when I first wanted to, none of this would have happened. My stubbornness was my undoing. You might as well know that last Wednesday night, Butch I had a big fight. He punched me in the chest, punched a hole in the wall, then left. That was the final straw. I know what you're thinking. It's about time, right? Well, when I started packing up his stuff I found some weird black book and," she lowered her voice to a whisper, "twenty thousand dollars."

Linda gasped. Mandy's mouth fell open. They both leaned in to hear more.

Elle repeated the story up to George getting shot. "So, we really don't know for sure who is after us or where they are now. That's why the police and the FBI are involved. George and I have been busy trying to stay out of sight, but not very well, obviously. It's all my fault. I wish I'd never laid eyes on Butch!" She waited for Mandy to say, "I told you so."   But there was silence. She looked over at her sister.

"Well?" she said to Mandy.

Mandy's eyes widened. "Well, what?"

"You're not going to say I told you so?"

Mandy smiled. "I could. But I think you've suffered enough. I don't need to say it."

Chapter 19

Mandy sipped her coffee. "I can't believe what you've been dealing with! I hardly know what to say. I can't believe Butch is dead! I wanted him to go away, but not like that! I agree his charm is what got him into trouble! It's a safe bet there were too many women and too many women dumped!"

Elle frowned. "Not that I'd know, but I'm sure he had quite a history. He didn't just wake up one day, open his mouth and shock everyone with his smooth talk. It seems like it would take some years of practice."

"I'm sorry, sis," Mandy patted Elle's hand.

Elle told them how she blamed herself for all his troubles. The girls were sympathetic.

Finally, Elle sighed and pulled her phone out of her purse. While the sisters waited, Elle pressed the keys. "Agent Travis? It's Elle Wickersham. Did you get the word that George Wendling was shot this afternoon? Yes. He is ok. He was shot in the thigh on the sidewalk outside the bowling alley. When the ambulance took him to OHSU, they let me go with him. The bullet nicked the femoral artery, so they had to call in a vascular surgeon. Yes. Since he lost so much blood, they had to transfuse him, but he did very well, and he is in recovery. We'll know more pretty soon. No. It's too early to tell. But he is very healthy. Dr Bennett did say that in 97% of cases like this the limb is saved.

I'm worried about his safety. Do you think he needs protection? I'm wondering if they meant to hit me. Yes. What? Say that again? No, I didn't. No one told us. Why? Would it be possible to have someone keep an eye on George? Well, yes, I know that. We rented a car. Oh! Which reminds me! We think we saw Butch's car driving around in that parking lot! Blue Camaro, license

SEXY1. Ok. I will. Thanks." Elle laid her phone down on the table. She looked at the sisters – hers and George's.

"Some dunderhead released Agent Carson from custody. Not enough evidence to hold him. He is a free man.
Total silence at the table.

Finally, Elle spoke. "Well, we have to leave sometime. It might as well be now."

Three subdued ladies walked out of the café, each brain wrestling with all the information just exchanged. There wasn't much conversation on the ride down in the elevator; each girl still trying to assimilate the shocking events of the past few days. When the doors opened, they said their good-byes and Mandy headed toward the parking garage elevators.

Elle realized she needed to get the rental from the bowling alley, so she called to Mandy who was just about to get in the elevator, to hold up for a moment. Linda asked Elle if she was coming back. Elle said yes, so Linda said she was going back to the surgery waiting area. Elle said she'd meet her there, but first she wanted to go get the car. Linda said ok and headed over to the surgery waiting area. Mandy waited at the elevator to find out what Elle needed so they didn't have to shout at each other.

"Oh, good. Sis, could you please take me to the bowling alley to pick up George's rental?"

Mandy nodded. "Sure, and then I need to go home. Sam has been out of town for two days. Are you ok with that? Do you have the key to the rental?"

Elle smiled. "Absolutely. Go be with your hubs. It's perfectly ok with me. Yes. The nurses in recovery gave me his wallet and keys."

The girls got in the elevator to the parking garage. They located Mandy's BMW and drove out into the evening sunset. Mandy expertly weaved her way in and out of traffic, as only an Oregonian can, until they arrived at the bowling alley. She had to drive around the parking lot several times to find the car, and eventually, she dropped Elle off at what they both hoped was the correct vehicle. She waited until Elle was actually in the car before she waved and drove away.

Elle maneuvered her way out of the very full parking lot and was finally on the road. She saw a Macy's, and without much thought, as though she were magnetized, turned into the parking lot. "If I still can't go home, I'd better stock up. And I should find a well-lit laundromat!"

She strolled around Macy's for some time until she found everything she needed for the next few days. Three pair of black pants, three shirts, another package of underwear, a new bra and another pair of flip flops, red with rhinestones on the strap. Then she decided while she was here, she might as well buy herself some work shoes. So, she picked out a pair of concourse shoes, and a pair of cute flats for flying. She could hear Butch in her head. "Why do you need another pair of concourse shoes? Your other pair looks like new. And besides, they're boring! Plain black high heels. All you do is wear them through the airport. When you get on the plane you change into flats!" It was quite pleasant to shop for herself without getting a lecture from Mr. Spend-Every-Dime.

Finished in Macy's she headed into the mall to look for some things for George. She entered the first bookstore that appeared in her sights and there she found a couple of crossword books and was happy to see two Felix Francis books she hadn't read. It still amazed her Dick's son could turn out great novels 99% as good as his. She was even more excited to see this place still carried the Fifth Avenue candy bar. For some reason it had been growing scarce. She added four bars to her pile and went to the register to check out. As she paid the bill she absently looked out into the mall. It was quiet. Not a lot of traffic this evening. She was fine with that. And no lawless profligates skulking out there that she could see. She had started to feel guilty about being so cavalier about her safety, but she rationalized it by telling herself that no criminal would be caught dead in Macy's.

Just to be safe, she stayed in groups of shoppers and waited to stroll out to the car with a group of about six people. She slid into the driver's seat with relief. Reasonably calm, she pointed the rental towards Dick's Sporting Goods.

She walked in and asked for directions to mace or pepper spray. The young man came out from behind the counter and took her to that section of the store. She'd never felt the need for something before now, but she was determined to stay safe. She picked up a cute object called the SABRE® Jogger Self Defense Pepper Gel. She read the explanation which said "fits in the palm of your hand, so it won't slow you down when running or walking. A hand strap allows for immediate deployment, allowing you to react quickly to a threat. A high-powered ballistic stream reduces wind blow back and reaches a twelve-foot range. This powerful gel dispenses up to thirty-five bursts at police strength." "Perfect," she thought. She picked two, one for back up, and returned to the checkout.

She returned to the car without incident and drove to the hospital. She parked in the garage and sneaked into the elevator. She had decided she was just going to pretend someone was watching her all the time and was, therefore, determined to be on her guard all the time.

She walked into the surgery waiting area and asked Florence if George was out of recovery. She looked at her list and told her he had been taken to his room on the 6th floor. Room 601, she told her. Elle thanked her and asked her if Linda, George's sister had been there.

"Oh!" Florence said. "She asked me to tell you she had gotten a migraine and needed to go home so if you would keep her posted, she'd appreciate it."

"Thank you for letting me know. I'm so sorry about Linda. Yes, I'll call her later or maybe in the morning. Thanks again." Elle hurried out into the hallway and headed for the elevator.

Still holding one of the pepper gels in her hand, she breathed a sigh of relief when she at last arrived in George's room. He was sleeping so she quietly arranged a chair close to his bed and sat down. She rested her elbows on the bed near his head, folded her arms, and put her head down. She closed her eyes and forced herself to relax.

She heard a cough and lifted her head.
He was awake. "Hi"

"Hi back. How do you feel?"

"With my fingers." He was a bit hoarse.

Elle groaned. "I knew you would say that. I almost said 'and don't say with your fingers!'"

George smiled groggily.

Elle felt the tears coming. "Oh, George, can you ever forgive me?"

George reached up and wiped a tear off her cheek. "Why are you saying that? There is nothing to forgive!"

"I nearly got you killed!"

"Sweetie, this is not your fault!"

"Oh yes, it is! If I'd left Butch when I first wanted to, this would never have happened!"

"We'll have no more of those kinds of thoughts. What's done is done. Let's not dredge up the past. I don't blame you. Not for one second. Do you read me?"

"I guess."

"Please believe me."

"Ok. I believe you."

"Do you?"

"Yes. Have I ever lied to you?"

"Yes. The adoption thing, remember? And when we were in the fourth grade, you told me our teacher, Miss Thornberg, was really a man."

Elle burst out laughing. "Oh dear, I was such a trial!"

"Actually," George put his hand on his forehead and sighed dramatically. "I don't know if I'll ever get over it. I was madly in love with her – him! I sobbed into my pillow every night for a week!" He sighed again.

"I really was kind of a brat! I'm sorry! But besides those two whoppers, have I ever lied any other times that you can think of?"

"Not at the moment, but I'll let you know if anything else comes to mind." He responded dryly.

Elle knew he was trying to cheer her up. George not only made everything more fun, but just being around him made her happy, even when he had just come out of surgery.

Chapter 20

Elle asked George if he felt like sitting up for a few minutes. He said, "Sure," and she pressed the button to raise the head of the bed. She helped him carefully scoot up, fluffed the pillows around him, and smoothed the sheet out over his leg, being very careful not to touch the surgery site.

When he was comfortable, she put all her purchases on the bed for him to see. "Cool! You found a Fifth Avenue! I wondered if they had quit making them. We might have to start hoarding them! And the Francis books. Cool! Can you believe Felix has turned out to be just as good as his dad?"

Elle looked pleased. "That's exactly what I was thinking!"

"Great minds!"

"Thanks, but you're the summa guy."

"Excuse me! That's MISTER Summa Cum Laude to you, girlie."

"Oh, dear, I beg your pardon! By the way, why aren't you in the Mensa Society?'

"Oh, you have to take an I.Q. test and the results have to be within the top 2% of all the scores. I just didn't feel like spending one to two hours taking a test."

"Really? One to two hours? I looked it up and some people get through the test in twenty minutes!"

George chuckled. "Well however long it takes, I just wasn't interested."

Elle thought his speech was slowing down. She picked up her phone and looked at the calendar. "By the way, speaking of your Alma Mater, the first Zag game is November first. Shall I see if I can get tickets?"

George grinned sleepily. "Do you know your schedule that far ahead? This is only September."

Elle noticed he was starting to fade out, but she said, "No but I'll arrange to trade with someone if you want to go."

"You had better try for tickets first. You know how that goes."

Elle sighed. "Yeah, I know. I think you should try to sleep".

George and Elle were Zag fans. They really hadn't had much choice. They were brought up on Zag basketball. Spokane was not only their fathers' hometown, but it was also home to Gonzaga University, which was home to the most amazing basketball team ever, the Bulldogs, coached by the amazing Mark Few. Anyone who lived for any length of time in Spokane couldn't help being a Gonzaga fan. So of course, Bob Wendling and Jim Wickersham were already hooked before they even entered Gonzaga. Moving to Portland didn't lessen their enthusiasm. They still followed the Zags and watched the games on TV. Ergo, basketball was sacred, which meant when the Zags were playing the families ended up at one house to watch. Just two rules: be there or have a darn good excuse, and no talking except during commercials. Occasionally the dads would get tickets to a home game, and they would all go to Spokane. It wasn't often because there were so many season ticket holders there wasn't enough space in the Kennel, which was the nickname for McCarthy Athletic Center.

When Bob and Jim were law students, Gonzaga was just beginning the climb to great heights. They both graduated in 1994 and it wasn't until 1999 when the Zags made a Cinderella run to the Elite Eight. Every year after that they appeared at the NCAA Tournament. They got better and better. In 2016–17, the Bulldogs went to their first Final Four in school history!

George and Elle had heard the stats so much they both could repeat them verbatim, but they were fans just like their parents.

George, eyelids at half-mast, was looking at all his loot. "Hey, I'm really loving all this stuff you brought. Did you bring me a pencil for the crosswords? Did you buy anything for yourself?"

Elle opened the bag and brought out a package of pencils, a sharpener and some eraser tops. "See? I'm just like a girl scout. I'm prepared! I love the smell of a freshly sharpened pencil. Yes, I did buy some things for myself. Pants, shirts, another package of underwear, a new bra and another pair of flip flops I couldn't resist! They're red with rhinestones on the strap – so cute! A pair of concourse shoes. Some cute flats for flying."

"Good. You definitely need more clothes." He chuckled faintly. "But I don't see why you need concourse shoes. All you do is wear them from the shuttle, through the airport. Then you all change into flats. But it's your money. You should get to spend it any way you like."

Elle's mouth fell open. "You are a man in a million! Thank you for remembering that! Could I get that in writing?" She yawned. "Oh, I'm so sorry!"

George yawned too. "It's contagious, but you should try to get some sleep, too. Where are you going to stay tonight?"

Elle grimaced. "I'm just going to go back to our hotel from last night. I don't feel like starting over again." She leaned down to kiss him on the forehead, but George put his arms up around her and kissed her on the lips. He lingered, and so did she. Then she did pull back. "This is weird."

"Weird but fun, right?" He was teasing her. "After a while, you'll come around to my way of thinking. You always do. I'm a force to be reckoned with!"

Elle rolled her eyes again. "Time to sleep."

He nodded. His eyes were already closed. She pressed the button to lower his head and helped him get comfortable, fluffed his pillows, and turned out the overhead light. She felt a great sense of relief as she left the room. She stopped in the hallway and again attached the pepper spray to her hand like it showed in the directions. She felt a whole lot safer with that gem.

In the parking garage, her flip flops slapping on the cement echoed through the silent building. It was well-lit so she could easily find her way to the car. She liked to look at license plates whenever she was in a parking lot or a garage. She had always done it. It was a habit. She absently read plates as she walked along. California, Washington, Oregon, Sexy1… She stopped. She backed up. She crept over to the car next to the Camaro. No one in the car. Where was he? Who is he? Who is driving Butch's car? Elle's heart was jumping up and down in her chest.

Chapter 21

Elle was frozen with fear. Her heart rate had sped up, and she felt weak in the knees. Is the person in the hospital visiting someone? Who would he be visiting? He wouldn't be visiting George. Would he? Why? Unless he wanted to kill him. That's stupid. Why would anyone want to kill George? What am I saying? They've already tried to kill George! Unless it was meant for me. Unless they think we have the book. But who?? If they think they can threaten me by killing George… they're right!

Elle turned around and ran back to the elevator. Waiting for it to arrive, she frantically dug in her purse for her phone. She pulled it out and dialed Agent Travis.

"Agent Travis! This is Elle Wickersham. I'm sorry to call you so late. I'm at the hospital. Butch's car is parked on the same level as mine, and there's no one in it. I'm frightened. Would you have any idea who is driving Butch's car? That's silly. Sorry. How would you know? It's so spooky! I am calm! Well, not really. I'm freaked out! Is there anything you can do? What? Ok. Ok. I'm so sorry. I'll be quiet and let you talk. Sorry."

She listened and began to relax. "Ok. Thank you so much. I'm still going back up to the room. Fine. I won't say anything. Thank you. Thank you."

She took her flip flops off as she left the elevator. She didn't want anyone to hear her. She moved as silently as possible down the corridor.

Elle stood outside George's room and listened. Silence. Then she heard footsteps. She looked around and saw some guy in a wrinkled suit walking toward her with a cup of coffee. She poked her head in the room and saw a man in jeans and a leather jacket at George's bedside. This was totally wrong. It's evening. Who makes rounds this time of night? No uniform. She stepped inside the doorway and said, "Hey!" The man turned around and came at her. He had something in his right hand. Some kind of cloth like a hanky. She screamed and attempted to run out of the room. The man caught her arm and suddenly she felt him let go. She fell backwards against the wall, opened her eyes and saw the wrinkled suit handcuffing the man and asking him what he was doing. Elle rushed over to George's bed. He was asleep. Something was wrong. He should have woken up when she screamed. She was now joined by two nurses whose faces registered shock and concern. Elle leaned down to George's face.

"Eww. He stinks!"

The wrinkled suit man's voice came from behind the nurses. "That's chloroform!"

One of the nurses told everyone to stand back. Elle looked at her name tag. It said Jeannie. The wrinkled suit man and Elle stepped back. Jeanie took George's vital signs and checked him over thoroughly. She turned to the younger nurse whose name tag said Hillary and told her to go prepare a dose of NAC. Hillary turned to hurry out of the room and Jeannie called after her, "140 mg please!" She heard Hillary, already back at the nursing station, say ok.

Elle looked anxiously at Jeannie. "Is he going to be ok?"

Jeannie nodded. "He didn't inhale much. I'm giving him a dose of N-acetylcysteine which we call NAC. 140 mg is just the standard dose for the antidote and just to be safe, we'll follow it up in four hours with a 70mg dose."

Hillary was back in no time, and she immediately injected the dose of NAC into George's IV.

Jeannie told Hillary thanks, and then she smiled and said to Elle, "While the right dose of chloroform soaked in a rag can definitely knock you unconscious, it would take much longer than what they show in movies. You wouldn't drop unconscious just by taking a whiff. With a perfectly measured dose, it would take at least 5 minutes to render someone unconscious."

George opened his eyes and tried to focus.

Elle looked at him anxiously. "How are you?"

George took a deep breath and coughed. "I think I need a mint. I've a funny taste in my mouth and my throat is a bit raspy."

Elle dug around in her purse and pulled out a tube of Mentos. She popped one out and handed it to him.

Jeannie fluffed up a very groggy George's pillows, got him tucked in and made sure he was comfortable. She asked George if he needed anything, and he said no.

"Oh, Jeannie," George said. "This is my friend, Elle." Elle smiled at her. "I can't tell you how much I appreciate your wonderful care of George."

Jeannie smiled back. "Well, he's a model patient. We're going to be sad to see him go!" She left the room and the wrinkled suit man stepped forward and spoke to George.

"Hi, I'm Sgt. Swanson with the Portland Police Bureau. Here's my ID" He held out his badge so they could all see. "I can see now why Agent Travis was so concerned about you," he said to George. "I'm really sorry I wasn't here sooner. I figured it was an ok time to go grab coffee. I've been up for forty-eight hours, and I really needed a boost. I won't make that mistake again! I'll wait for my replacement. We dodged a bullet there – oops! That wasn't a very smart thing to say, was it? Sorry about that."

Elle mentally forgave him entirely for his wrinkled suit, especially when she remembered she had been sleeping in her clothes for the past week. She told him not to worry. It was a natural thing to say. "But if you leave your post again, I personally will find you and strangle you. By the way," she looked over at the leather jacket guy handcuffed to the bed rail of the other empty bed in George's room, "What are you going to do with that guy?"

Sgt. Swanson looked over at the leather jacketed guy. "Well, this lucky guy is going to be picked up by my friends from the PPB and taken downtown to be interviewed, and maybe have a vacation at the Graybar Hotel!"

George was feeling more alert, and gingerly scooted himself up in the bed so he could join in the conversation. "So, Sergeant, got any news for us?"

Sgt. Swanson moved closer to the bed and said to George, "Agent Travis called me. He's coming in tomorrow morning to talk to both of you. He has information to share."

Elle yawned. "So, Sergeant, I'm not sure how much of this case you know, but the only reason I came rushing back up here is I saw my ex-boyfriend's car parked in the parking garage and he was killed a few nights ago. I couldn't understand how it's been being driven around town. I called Agent Travis and told him, so he knows. You probably should be aware too. It's a brand-new Blue Camaro, License SEXY1. I've decided I'm not leaving so I'll be here in the morning, too." She reached out and pressed the call button. When the nurse came in, it was Hillary. Elle asked her if it would be ok to spend the night. Hillary told her she was welcome. Then she said she'd be right back.

In a moment she came back with a fold up cot with sheets and a blanket. She opened up the cot and smoothly and efficiently made the bed up in about five seconds flat. She added an extra blanket at the foot, then handed Elle a box, which Elle opened to reveal minis of toothpaste, toothbrush, mouth wash, shampoo, conditioner, soap, comb, brush and deodorant.

Elle hugged the box. "This is so cute! Thank you!"
"Oh," Hillary said, "I've ordered breakfast for you. I just duplicated George's order. Is that ok? We can change it if you want."

Elle looked at George. "Bagels, cream cheese, coffee?"
Hillary and George both laughed.

Hillary looked at Elle. "You must have ESP!"

Elle chuckled. "No, we just know each other really well. And Hillary, thank you so much for all your kindness to us!"

Hillary smiled. "It's a pleasure! Please ring if you need anything," and she silently left the room.

Elle pulled a chair close to George's bed. "Are you ok?" He smiled. "I don't seem to be any worse for wear. I feel ok. So, I guess no damage was done."

Elle teared up. "This is so awful. How did we ever end up in this situation? How could I have been so stupid? I should have stayed far, far away from Butch! I knew he was bad news. Mandy told me from the very beginning he was going to be trouble. Gahh!"

George reached out and wiped away her tears. "Listen, can we change our past? No. So why waste energy fussing about something we cannot control? Let's just think about the future and how we're going to get through this. And please, sweetie, no more talk about anything being your fault."

She sighed. "I'll try."

"I'll count on it."

"Did you hear Agent Travis is coming in the morning to give us an update? Maybe he's got some good information."

George yawned. "I hope so. I need some good news."

Elle pulled the sheet up to his chin. "You need to sleep." She turned out the overhead light.

George grabbed her arm and pulled her down so he could kiss her.

"Now I can sleep," he whispered.

Elle peeked out into the hallway to see if Sgt. Swanson was out there. He gave her a salute. She waved back at him and feeling relieved he was there, she lay down on the cot and wondered how on earth they were going to get through this ordeal and maintain their sanity or, worse, their lives.

Chapter 22

Monday morning Elle's hearing woke up first. She lay there on her cot realizing someone had covered her up during the night. Her eyes still shut, she listened to a lecture on the correct way to repair a vascular bleed.

"The ballistic examination of the wound involves the description of three basic elements: the inlet, the outlet and the path…"
Elle opened her eyes. She stayed where she was and furtively looked around the room.

"These elements vary according to the weapon, the ammunition, the distance of fire but especially according to the crossed tissues. The damage incurred by the projectile energy is explained by crushing, laceration and stretching phenomena…"

Elle counted. Eleven. Eleven doctors standing around George's bed. An older doctor was the one doing the talking.

"Pre-hospital care remains a challenge. Stopping bleeding and rapid transportation of the wounded to a specialized center is the cornerstone of this phase…"

Elle wondered what George was thinking and how he was liking being the center of attention.

"Ballistic vascular injuries were generally encountered during wars. Armed conflicts have contributed significantly to the evolution of vascular surgery in general and to the development of many strategies for the management of ballistic injuries in particular, especially in the United States. Firearm injuries were rare in Tunisia until the outbreak of the revolts of the Arab countries. Remember, patients operated on for vascular trauma by firearms must always be reported. Here we have a young man who presented with a bullet wound to the thigh. Arterial revascularization was performed urgently. And the patient did well."

Dr Bennett was evidently finished, so he opened it up for questions. George was quiet and compliant as they observed the dressing change. There were a lot of questions and discussion.

Finally, rounds in this patient's room had come to an end and the herd moved on to the next one on the list. Some of the doctors, students, Elle presumed, looked at her and waved good-bye.

When the coast was clear, Elle, crawled out of her cot and headed to George's private restroom with her cute box of mini toiletries. She brushed her teeth and combed her wild blonde curls and told herself she could have a shower later today.

When she exited the bathroom, breakfast had arrived. She was starving! She sat down beside George's bed. The nurse had already been in to help him get ready for breakfast. She had also borrowed the tray table from the other bed and set up Elle's breakfast tray for her.

While they were eating, Agent Travis arrived. "Sorry to bust in on you guys so early but I need to get to work."

Elle offered to ring for coffee, but he declined with thanks.

"So, here's the deal. Butch was spending a lot of time in the bar at Berlusconi. He and the bartender are friends. We've had Berlusconi under surveillance for a long time, especially after we discovered that Dan – or Danny, is suspected of ties with the Mafia, and is the owner.

Elle's and George's mouths both dropped open.

George said, "Do you mean Agent Carson?"

"Agent Dan Carson of the FBI?" Elle echoed.

"Sad to say, but yes." Agent Travis continued. "We've never been able to pin anything on him because he keeps himself separated from the routine operation. Tony Romano and Franco Rossi – you call them Mutt and Jeff – work for him and they're the ones that hired Butch. Alonzo Bianchi is your shooter. That's your guy from yesterday, by the way. He is Danny's professional hired gun. Oh, speaking of guns, check this out!"

He reached down and pulled his left pant leg up and removed a gun from his ankle holster. "Ok, George, I know you like guns, and for just a moment I'm a happy civilian showing off my new toy, ok?"

George was curious. "So, we're supposed to pretend you didn't just do this?"

"Exactly." Agent Travis held it up for George and Elle to see. "It's brand new. It's a Walther Q4SF. Isn't that a nice piece of hardware?"

Elle, who was not a fan of guns, said weakly, "It's very pretty."

George was impressed. "Hey, I need one of those!"
Elle frowned at him, but she knew better than to say anything. All the men in her family, and George's, were hunters and they loved guns, so she kept quiet.

"Anyway," Agent Travis said, "back to what I was saying. We have no proof, as of yet, but we think on top of everything else, Butch and his charming personality were very busy recruiting call girls to make some extra cash -- and they're working right out of the back of Berlusconi. The bartender was paying Butch in weed as well as cash." Agent Travis stopped talking. Elle and George were silent.

Elle couldn't speak. Her mind had frozen. She looked at George. He had nothing to say either.

Finally, Elle, her voice shaky, asked, "Is that all?"

Agent Travis shook his head. "There's more."

Elle nearly choked on her coffee. "M-m-more? What could there possibly be? What could be worse?"

Detective Travis looked at her sympathetically. "I'm sorry. This has been really hard on you. But it might comfort you to know we've matched the bullets from Butch and George. They both came from the same gun. And now that we have Alonzo in custody, we're just waiting for ballistics to confirm the bullets came from his gun.

The atmosphere in the room was silent shock.

Detective Travis stood up. "My friend, Agent Ken Summers, is part of the FBI team watching Berlusconi. They have photos of Butch coming and going with several different, incredibly beautiful young women. They also have photos of your Mutt and Jeff entering and leaving quite often. They're still hoping to connect Dan/Danny with the operation, but so far, he's been smart enough to stay hidden. They've also seen Alonzo a few times, but not often.

He leaned down and patted Elle on the shoulder. "I'm sorry, Elle."

She looked up at him and gave him a brave smile. "Thanks, Agent Travis, for being straight with us and keeping us in the loop."

He gave a small salute to George and disappeared down the hall.

Elle sighed and wondered for the hundredth time when this was going to end. And how it would end. She put her hands on her thighs and pushed herself to a standing position. "I feel like I'm a hundred years old."

George put his arms out and she went to him and let him hug her. It was comforting, and warm. "You're the most beautiful hundred-year-old I've ever seen."

She stepped back and grinned, "Just how many beautiful hundred-year-old women have you seen? I need more coffee. I'm going downstairs to the Espresso Bar. Do you want one?"

"Sure."

"Two Caramel Macchiatos?"

George gave her a thumbs up.

As she went into the hallway she checked for Sgt. Swanson or his replacement. There was someone sitting in Sgt. Swanson's chair.

She stopped to talk. "Are you the replacement?"

He nodded and said Sgt. Swanson would be back and there would be another officer working with them too.

Elle stood there a minute. "I'm sorry, but I'd feel a lot better if I could see your ID."

"Of course!" He stood up and pulled out his badge.

"Harold Pullman," Elle read out loud. "Thank you, Officer Pullman, for being here to help us. Do you know who that other officer will be? I'm kinda nervous."

Officer Pullman put his ID back in his pocket. "I'll find out and make sure they all show you their ID"

Elle took a breath. "I really appreciate that. Thank you."

Downstairs at the coffee bar she ordered drinks for herself and George and waited while the cute barista prepared them. As she said yes to whipped cream, she promised herself she'd start cutting back the calories but right now it was all about comfort. When she arrived back at George's room, Linda was there. George was signing papers, dealing with mail, giving her instructions, and generally catching up on work.

"Oh, Linda, how is your head? Would you like coffee? I'd love to get you some."

"Well, thank you! I'm a lot better this morning. Thank you, sweetie. Coffee would be lovely, if you don't mind?

"No, not at all. What would you like?"
She sighed. "I always get a skinny. Let's get wild today though. How about Caramel Macchiato? George always gets them and I'm always jealous."

Elle smiled. "Here you go! Just what the doctor ordered!"

"Is that yours? I couldn't take yours!"

"Don't be silly. I haven't touched it and its silly for that one to just sit there! It's yours!"

"Well, ok! Thanks!"

Elle left to go get another coffee. She met Sgt. Swanson coming on duty. "Hi! Good morning! Can I get you a coffee? I'm going down to the Espresso Bar."

"Hey, that would be great! Thanks! How about a Breve with a shot of peppermint? Thanks!"

"And by the way, I'm checking everyone's ID this morning so just for the record, may I see yours?"

Sgt. Swanson chuckled. "Of course. It's good you're being careful, especially after yesterday!" he showed Elle his badge and ID and she squinted at it closely.

"Good! I feel better now!" She smiled and thanked him.

"Absolutely! See you when you get back! Thanks again for the coffee!" Sgt. Swanson went off to relieve Harold.
Elle chuckled to herself. "Boy I'm getting a lot of steps today. I could hit my 10,000 just going for coffee!"

Back with two more coffees, she handed one to Sgt. Swanson and walked into George's room just as Linda was finishing up. And some flowers had been delivered. How nice. She walked over to see who sent them. She couldn't find a card.

"George, who brought the flowers?"

George shrugged. "Someone from Florence's staff."

Elle examined the bouquet. "Did Florence say who delivered them?

"No, she just said it was anonymous."

"Hmmm… weird. They're probably bugged." She winced, but she really was feeling suspicious. "I hate this feeling. Like I need to look over my shoulder. I wish this was all over!"

George agreed. "It's like living in a cage."

Chapter 23

Elle looked at the flowers again. She peered closer looking for some kind of identification telling her where they came from. She looked around the sides of the vase and lifted it up to look underneath. She even pulled the pot away from the decorative paper to see if there was anything on the vase itself. Just a sticky oval which suggested the removal of the tell-tale sticker. Elle chided herself she was getting paranoid. But who would go to that much trouble to stay anonymous? Seems a silly thing to do unless it was critical to not be recognized. She replaced the bouquet and fluffed it up to make it look as if it hadn't just endured molestation.

She paced back and forth in the room. She looked at George. He had dozed off. She paced some more. Finally, she called Mandy and asked her if she could meet for dinner. Mandy said yes and they arranged to meet.

Elle was feeling generous, so she said to her sis, "We don't have to do the Thirsty Lion. You choose."

Mandy stifled a laugh and thought a minute. Then she suggested the Chart House, her favorite for dinner.

Elle liked that suggestion. "Yum! Ok. Six-ish?"

"Perfect! See you tonight!"

Elle went out in the hall to talk to Sgt. Swanson. She told him the flowers made her nervous and to please be vigilant. He promised.

Sgt. Swanson stood up. "I think I might make some inquiries and see if I can find out who bought the flowers."

"That would be amazing! Thanks so much!" Elle was grateful. It was with a lighter step she went back into George's room.

She still felt restless and decided to take a walk down to the end of the hall to the public waiting room. She went in and stood in front of the windows looking out over the city. What a spectacular view, she thought. She stayed a few minutes longer and then returned to George's room.

When they brought George's lunch, the nurse asked her if she wanted something. She said no. "I might sneak down and get another turkey, cream cheese, cranberry sandwich. The one I had yesterday was really good."

She spent the afternoon with George while he was alternately partially awake and then dozing. She worked on some crossword puzzles in George's book and did some dozing herself. The physical therapist and his assistant came in to make George walk up and down the hall. They got him to his feet while Elle cringed. He looked really pale. They put a walker out for him, and he held on tight. They put the gait belt around his waist so they could catch him if he started to get weak in the knees. Then out they went. Elle stood in the doorway gritting her teeth. It looked painful. They didn't go far, but she thought it was too far. But he persevered. He arrived back, smiling and sweating. They got him tucked back in bed again and he breathed a great sigh of relief. She told George she was feeling antsy, so she was going to meet Mandy for dinner.

George said he thought that would be a good idea. "I'm sort of stuck here, but you keep forgetting you're free to come and go."

Elle grinned. "It's no fun out there without you."

The sun was a ball of fire on the horizon as she drove up to the Chart House. There was a pink tint everywhere. The view was second to none. From its vantage point at the top of historic Terwilliger Boulevard, Chart House seafood restaurant boasts some of the city's best views. Overlooking the gorgeous Willamette River and offering views of Mt. Hood, Mt. St. Helens and Mt. Adams on a clear day, it's one of the most majestic viewpoints in all of the Pacific Northwest.

She parked and walked in. When the sisters were seated, Elle looked around in awe. "I'd forgotten this spectacular view! No wonder this is your favorite! And by the way, this is my treat. I owe you. I should have listened to you a long time ago about Butch, and I just want to say I'm sorry for what I put you guys through. So, have whatever you like. Is one of your favorites still the Hazelnut Crusted Mahi Mahi? And Chocolate Lava Cake for dessert? We're splurging because I need a distraction."

Mandy lit up. "I'm totally on board, and yes those are my choices for dinner tonight!"

When the drinks waiter appeared, Mandy asked for white wine and Elle asked for a Margarita.

Elle chuckled. "I know. Weird. I'm not even having Mexican food! And what's worse I'm having Mud Pie for dessert. Those two things don't go together! Evidently, I'm ordering backwards. Now to decide what to have first." Elle studied the menu. Once or twice, she looked up from the menu to gaze out of the huge window to admire the scenery.

Mandy brought her back to reality. "How is George? I had lunch with Linda today. We were going to invite you, but we didn't think you would leave George."

"You're right. I didn't want to leave him, but I suddenly got a case of cabin fever and I decided I needed some fresh air. I can't sleep on that cot another night. I need to go back to the hotel room."

The waiter returned with their drinks, and Elle licked the salt off of a spot on the rim of her glass.

Mandy tested her wine. "Do you want to stay with us?"
"Thanks, but I don't want you to be in jeopardy. I probably shouldn't even be seen with you. When you go home just take the long way and dawdle."

"Boy, cloak and dagger stuff!"

The server appeared to take their order. She looked at Mandy with recognition. "Mrs. Phillips!"

Mandy looked up and smiled. "Hello, Brenda. So nice to see you again. I think we are ready. This is my sister, Elle."

Elle smiled. "How can you get any work done with a view like this?"

Brenda laughed. "Sadly, I don't have time to look out the window up here. It's always so busy!"

Brenda took their orders. Mandy gave hers, and then Elle decided on the filet mignon. She made sure Brenda got the order for Mud Pie.

Elle grinned at Brenda. "Don't tell anyone we're having Mud Pie. We're pretending we're health food nuts."

Brenda mimed the zipping of the lips and went to put the orders in.

As soon as Brenda left, Elle responded to the cloak and dagger comment. "Yeah, it's terrible. And speaking of that, I got a big earful from the detective handling the case. I hope it's ok to tell you this stuff. He didn't tell me not to, and you probably won't be as shocked as I was, but there are some things that will make your hair stand on end. I hope you can handle it. Or maybe I just shouldn't tell you."

"Well, you have to tell me now. I'm hooked!"

"Ok. Here goes". As Elle brought Mandy up to date, she again watched Mandy's face change expressions like a speeded-up video. Shock, anger, sadness, shock, astonishment, unbelief. It was all in her face, just as Elle's had been.

When she finished, Mandy was speechless. Elle wasn't surprised at that. It was the same reaction as hers. And what was there to say? It was beyond anything they had ever experienced. In fact, it reminded Elle of one of their mother's favorite expressions: 'It's out of the realm of my understanding' she'd say when something shocked her.

"You know," Elle said, "people say when you get married, you're not marrying the family, you're just marrying the person, but that is so wrong! Life is so much easier if the person you choose integrates really well with the family. I know it's not a law, but if a person is thinking about getting married, they should bring the groom to be – or the bride to be – around the family so the person can see firsthand how they get along with your family. Butch was so awful when it came to family stuff. He was so obnoxious and selfish and didn't even try. Everyone else tried really hard and that was so embarrassing for me. That's why we quit going to the family stuff. I just couldn't torture our families, that is George's family and our family, anymore!"

Mandy laid her hand, palm down, on the middle of the table. Elle reached out and put her hand over Mandy's. Mandy smiled and said, "And you never knew how painful it was for George."

Elle squeezed Mandy's hand. "I'm beginning to. I was really blind. There he was all the time. Patiently waiting for me to come to my senses."

Mandy shook her finger at Elle. "He used to cry on my shoulder and beg me to tell you to dump the current boy."

"Poor George. He should hate me by now. But he doesn't seem to."

Mandy sipped her wine. "So, are you dealing with all of this ok? I mean with Butch getting killed?"

Elle smiled. "You don't have to worry about me. This past year has been a struggle. I finally did some reading about manic depression. I mean bipolar disorder. Butch was textbook! One of the items was shopping sprees. You know he couldn't keep a dime in his pocket. Any time he had money he'd spend it. On stupid stuff. Toys and candy and candles. He was obsessed with candles. He even gambled away one of my paychecks. Did I ever tell you that?"

Mandy's shock was all too evident. "No! You didn't tell me! How did he get your paycheck?"

"It was before they switched to automatic payroll deposit. I was in a hurry, so I endorsed my check and asked Butch to deposit it. Big mistake."

Elle really needed this sister time. Mandy talked about her job and how busy they were. Elle never had known exactly what Mandy did. She just knew she worked for the hospital and worked in the Medical Education Office and did something to manage all the new interns every fall. They talked about the two families and about ski season coming up. Elle mentioned how much easier it was going to be without dragging Butch along.

She contemplated for a moment. "You know, I've felt absolutely nothing for him for a long time now. Long before he died. He had become an albatross around my neck. That's why I asked for the Australia run. That gave me seventeen hours I didn't have to see or hear from him. Plus the time it took me to get to my flight or get home, since Qantas doesn't fly to Portland right now. I have to go from Portland to Dallas to get to my flight. That was giving me a lot of alone time. I was beginning to dread coming home. I just don't want to live like that. I'm sorry to sound so callous, but it's a relief to not have Butch in my life anymore. So many things sucked the energy out of me. That incessant talking! I never knew anyone who could talk continuously for hours! It was like the only time he was silent was when he was asleep! I never wished him dead, though."

The sun slowly sank, and the sky changed colors in a panorama of blues and pinks to yellows and purples, then it was evening, and the lights of the city twinkled like a fairyland.

Brenda delivered the bill and told them she was their cashier. Elle was ready for it so she stuck her credit card in the slot and handed it right back. Mandy got ready to leave. "I need to go. I haven't seen Sam very much since he got home, but if you need me, I'll come, ok?"

They both stood up and hugged. "Love you, Sis," said Mandy in Elle's ear. "Thanks for dinner."

"Love you too," Elle replied. "Thanks for the sister time! You go on ahead. I'm going to dawdle." She sat down again and waited for her credit card while Mandy rushed away.

Brenda brought her credit card and receipt. Elle signed the restaurant copy, added a large tip, and stuck it back inside the folder. She sat for a minute watching the night sky and the tiny diamonds far below. Such a beautiful show, she thought.

Elle actually felt rejuvenated and ready to deal with whatever was ahead, as she walked out to the car. Sitting in the driver's seat, she located her phone in her purse and called the hospital. She asked for George's room and in a few moments was relieved to be speaking with George.

"Oh good, someone hasn't kidnapped you or done something terrible to you!"

George smiled. "Nope. They're pretty nice so far! How is your sister?"

"We had a nice time and we had great food. I shouldn't be telling this to someone who is eating hospital food."

"It's ok. I can take it. Are you coming up?"

"No. If you don't mind too much, I'm going to the hotel room. I'll call you again from there and let you know where I am."

"Ok, Sweetie. Please be observant."

"I promise. Talk to you soon."

She hung up and drove out of the parking lot. She returned to the hotel, wearily dropped her shopping bags on George's bed and pulled out a new black night shirt. Then she sat on the edge of the bed and called George.

When he answered, she said, "Whew! Good! You're there."

He smiled and asked, "Where else do you think I'd be?"

"Just happy to know you're where you're supposed to be!" She told him where she was and she was going to crawl between the sheets and sleep for a week. "Not really, I'll be back in the morning."

She was so tired. She lay back just for a minute and shut her eyes. Weird dreams assailed her until she woke fully clothed and sweating. Looking at the clock which showed two a.m. she decided to put her night shirt on. Off with her clothes, on with the shirt, and this time under the covers in about a minute flat.

Chapter 24

She was wide awake at five o'clock Tuesday morning. So much for sleeping in. Disgusted, she crawled out of bed and staggered toward the coffee maker. In a minute or so, there was coffee. Powdered creamer. Ugh. Oh well. Desperate times call for desperate measures. Or however that goes.

The shower felt really good. She dressed and felt human. Another cup of coffee should seal the deal. Or better yet, coffee at the hospital espresso bar.

On her way out she asked if her room was available for another night and was told yes. She asked them if she could keep it until the end of the week. The desk agent checked and said it would be fine. Good! As she walked out to her car the bright September sunshine warmed her up and sent a few rays into her heart. A beautiful fall day in Portland! She was glad to be alive!

She went through the McDonald's drive thru and got two McGriddles© with sausage and cheese and a small diet soda to wash them down. She ate one on the way to the hospital and decided to stick the other one in her purse and save it for George.

She was humming as she got off the elevator on George's floor. Her flip flops made slapping noises in the early morning quiet. Most of the patients were still sleeping peacefully, cozy and warm, until their doctors showed up on their rounds with their stethoscopes fresh from the freezer.

Something was not right. Ahead on the chair outside George's door was the person who was keeping an eye on George. Why was he asleep? He was bent over with his chin on his chest. She was going to smack him in the head and tell him he was fired!

"Excuse me. Wakey wakey!" She tapped him on the shoulder. He didn't wake up. His body rolled off the chair onto the floor. There was a knife stuck into his back between his shoulder blades.

Elle stood frozen in shock. She couldn't believe she was looking down at another dead body! She ran into George's room. Empty bed. "George?" She went and looked in the bathroom. Fear was bubbling inside her like a poison stew.

She ran down to the nurse's station. Relieved to see it was Jeannie, a nurse she had met, she blurted out, "Jeannie, there is a dead body in the hall, and George is not in his room!

Jeannie jumped up and ran the short distance to George's room. She knelt down to look at the body. Elle stood back giving her room. Jeannie felt for a pulse and agreed the person was dead.

Elle pulled her cell phone out and called Agent Travis. Trying not to cry she told him what had happened. As she talked the tears rolled, and she had trouble making herself understood. When she ended the call, she told Jeannie she'd called the FBI agent they'd been communicating with.

Jeannie said, "That's good. I'm going to make a couple of calls and I'll be right back." Another nurse arrived with a sheet to cover the body. Jeannie returned to the nurses' station and made two phone calls. Then she walked back down to where Elle was standing. "I called the ER, and a doc is going to come up and pronounce. Then I called security to contact the police and come up. I'm so sorry. I have no idea where Mr. Wendling could be. He has no tests this morning, so he has no reason to be out of his room! And he can't walk without crutches, or a cane, and they're all right here in his room. I don't know what to tell you. Frankly, I don't know where he is! This is just dreadful! In all my years of patient care, this has never happened. I'll go and talk with some of the staff. The night shift is just going off duty, so I'll check with them." Jeannie brought a chair out into the hall for Elle to sit. She sat down. She felt like a bag of cement. Exhausted. Unable to think.

Agent Travis arrived followed by police officers and forensics, Elle guessed. He gently steered Elle down further toward the end of the hall to the public waiting area to be out of the way so the forensics team could get started. Then he sat with her. She told him exactly what had transpired from the time she left the elevator. Agent Travis made copious notes. When they were finished, he asked her if she wanted to go back to her hotel.

"I don't know. I think I want to stay here in case he's still here in the building."

One of the detectives stuck his head out of the room and called down to the agent. "Agent Travis, can I see you for a moment?"

Agent Travis went back toward George's room to listen to the detective. Then he came back to where Elle was waiting. "The guys watching Berlusconi saw two men, one tall, one short, deliver what they thought was laundry to the back door about 4:00 a.m. There easily could have been a body in the cart. They didn't want to blow their cover, so they didn't get a good look.

Elle ran her cold clammy fingers through her curls. "Well, that would make sense, because the night staff does rounds about 3 AM. And that's the last time until just before report."

Agent Travis looked puzzled. "Report?"

"Yes," Elle said. "It's where both shifts meet, and the departing shift informs the arriving shift about every patient and what happened during the night."

Agent Travis made a phone call. "Hey, this is Travis. I want an APB on Tony Romano and Franco Rossi and make sure we still have Alonzo in custody. Thanks!"

To Elle, "We've got Alonzo and we'll have those two pretty soon."

Elle's cell phone rang. She saw it was Linda. She answered with, "Hi! What are you doing up this time of day?"

Linda talked and Elle listened. Elle's face did vignettes of emotions from smiling to astonishment. Elle told Linda she'd call her back in a few minutes and to stay there. She didn't want to say anything about George's absence until she had more information, and she was calm, whenever that might be, she thought dryly.

When she disconnected from Linda, she told Agent Travis some flowers had come to George's office and this time there was a card. She looked him in the eye. "It said 'You can have George back when we get the book.' Agent Travis!" Elle said a little too loudly. "They have George!"

Chapter 25

Agent Travis put his fingers to his lips to tell her to be quiet. He got on his phone and made a call. "Hey, it's pretty likely George is being held at Berlusconi. So have your guys be extra vigilant. I'm going to get a search warrant.

Elle jumped up. Trying to make herself relax and be calm, she began pacing the length of the waiting area and back. She looked at Agent Travis, but he was looking at his notes. She walked pretty fast a few times, but she finally slowed down a bit and then stopped. She sat back down in the chair by Agent Travis. She put her hands over her face to cover the tears.

Agent Travis stood up to leave the room. "Hang in there. We'll get George back." As always, he patted her shoulder. "I promise I'll call you the minute I know something. We have people combing the hospital just to make sure he's not stashed somewhere in the building, and the guys watching the restaurant are on high alert." He smiled at her and disappeared into the hallway.

Hillary walked in, sat down with her and put her arm around Elle. "I heard in report about George. I'm so sorry! Nothing like this has ever happened in any hospital where I've been employed! It's terrible! Everyone is in shock!"

"Thanks, Hillary. I'm not sure what to do. Should I pack up George's things? Or should I leave everything like it is?"

"Well, technically, he hasn't been discharged, so he's still a patient here… It's kind of a weird situation, but if the police – I mean WHEN the police find him, they need to bring him back so we can look him over and make sure no further damage been done to his leg. I think you should just leave everything as it is."

"Fine with me. Thank you. You have my number on file if you need to talk to me."

"Yes, now try not to worry." Hillary frowned. "Oh, that was stupid." They hugged and Hillary returned to her duties.

Elle decided to go back to the hotel. She picked up her purse headed purposefully toward the elevator, ignoring the representation of various law enforcement branches studiously concentrating on their crafts. She noticed more medical personnel had come to pick up the body.

Back in her hotel room, she paced. She called Linda. She gently explained everything and told her she'd keep her posted. Linda hung up crying. She called Mandy, who was horrified. "Do you want me to come and sit with you?"

"I dunno. I don't know what I want." She dabbed her eyes with a damp tissue. "No. I'll call you if I need you to come hold my hand, but right now I'm terrible company."

She lay on the bed and stared at the ceiling. "Oh, George, where are you? Please be ok." The tears rolled down into her ears. "Please, dear Lord, protect George wherever he is. I don't deserve your help. I only talk to you when I need something, and I know better. But I know you care about us, in spite of how human we are. So, if it's in your plan, please keep him alive!" She dabbed her eyes and her ears, same damp tissue. She sat up tossing it in the trash can.

She called Mandy. "Can you meet me for a cup of coffee?" "Absolutely. Do you want me to take the day off?"

Elle shrugged. "I dunno. My brain is scrambled. I don't know what I want."

"Why don't you come here to my office, and we'll go up to third floor again. I can spend the whole day with you or whatever you feel like."

"Perfect. See you there. Thanks, sis."

Elle went down to the lobby and asked the concierge to get her a cab. It took just a few minutes, and he was walking her out to the sidewalk and helping her into a taxi. When the taxi pulled up in front of the hospital, she paid the driver and headed toward the front doors. Entering the familiar building brought tears afresh. She fished in her purse for some tissues. At the entrance to Mandy's office, she wiped her eyes once more and blew her nose.

Mandy was on the phone, so Elle sat and waited. As Mandy was finishing her call, she frowned at Elle's puffy eyes and red nose. Mandy grabbed her purse and tidied her desk and the two girls walked to the elevators. When they arrived at the café Elle decided she might eat something but not yet. She poured herself some coffee and grabbed a couple of creamers. She hadn't kept track of Mandy, so she just went through the line to pay. When she got to the cashier, the cashier said her coffee had been paid for. Elle looked around and saw Mandy was already at a table and she was waving at her. She thanked the cashier and went and sat down with Mandy.

Elle sighed. "Thanks for the coffee."

Mandy looked at her sympathetically. I feel so bad for you. I just wanted to treat you!"

Elle took a sip of the hot liquid. Nectar of the Gods, she thought. She leaned forward a little so she wouldn't have to shout. "Agent Travis is on the job. He seems very efficient and capable. I just wish I could find George myself. Of course, that's all they need to impede their investigation – some stupid girl getting in their way and gumming up the works. And I feel so guilty! This is all my fault! Butch is dead and he's still giving us grief!"

"Boy, little did I know last Wednesday what was ahead, that I'd be in the middle of a huge drama with Butch dead and George missing." Elle wiped her eyes with her napkin. Linda was telling me that very day, Wednesday, she was going shopping this weekend and lunch at the Thirsty Lion. I said I'd go. What a difference a day makes! I think she was planning on asking you, too." Elle sighed again.

Mandy nodded. "Yeah, she asked me to go too. But no one's in the mood to have a shopping day out."

Elle smiled sadly. "They've been shopping, but it was for me because I haven't been able to go home."

Mandy patted Elle's hand. "No, that's not the fun kind of shopping."

"I know you haven't wanted to talk to the folks for fear of upsetting them even more, but they send their love and prayers."

"Dad gave Linda money to give to George. "He's been paying for everything. He's so funny. It's hard for him to let a girl pay." Elle chuckled.

"Last of the dying breed, gallantry." Mandy sighed. "There are few left on the planet. But, in the interest of fairness, I should qualify that with the sad fact money is hard to come by these days, and you have to be a two-career family if you want to get ahead – or stay even. So, do you want me to spend the day with you? Or shall I go back to work? Or what do you wish?"

Elle sighed. "I dunno. I've no idea what I want. Well, I want George back. Why don't you go ahead and go back to work, and I'll call you if I need you. OK?

Mandy put her arm around Elle and said, 'OK, if you're sure."

They got off the elevator on the main floor and hugged. Mandy headed back toward her office and Elle walked out of the hospital and stood looking for a cab. A black limousine rolled slowly by, as if someone was searching for an address or something. She saw the cabs parked down the street, so she raised her arm to hail the cab. Suddenly, arms swooped her up and before she could scream, she was in the back seat of the limo with a gloved hand over her mouth. Panic rose up in her throat like acid reflux and she thought she might throw up.

Then the gloved hand was off, and she was breathing in through her nose and out of her mouth to keep from vomiting. Her stomach was lurching. The limo moved sleekly down the street. She leaned back in her seat and tried to calm down. She hated throwing up almost as much as whoever was doing this to her. When she decided she wasn't going to do that horrible thing she hated so much, she turned to look at her captor. It was Mutt, the stupid goon from the other day. She glared at him, "What do you think you're doing? You have some nerve! Stop this car at once and let me out!"

Mutt grinned broadly showing cigarette-stained teeth. He was still in his 1920's outfit. She tried to see through the tinted glass and wondered if it was "Jeff" doing the driving.

"Hey, I'm just following orders." Mutt's breath was about to send the contents of her stomach onto the upholstery of this very nice vehicle.

She took a deep breath through her nose. "Whose orders are you following?" she asked slyly.

"My boss, of course." Mutt answered stupidly.

"Where is George?" she shouted at him. "What have you done with him? Is he alive?" Suddenly she was furious. "Tell me where he is!" She shouted right in Mutt's face.

"What's going on back there? Can't you control her?" Jeff was yelling too.

Mutt put his hands over his ears. "It's so noisy! She's yelling in my face!"

"Do I have to stop this car and come back there?" Jeff yelled. "Get on with it! Tell her to give us the book! Do I have to do everything myself?" Jeff kept looking back at Mutt. It was making Elle nervous because he wasn't watching the road. Elle watched the nose of the car wander across the line.

"Watch where you're going!" Elle screamed. She shut her eyes. She grabbed the handle over the window and hung on. She felt the car twist and then there was an almighty crash. Then silence.

Chapter 26

She opened one eye. It looked like they were actually parked on the sidewalk. She didn't feel bad. No broken bones. She let go of the handle and sat forward. Still ok. She opened her door carefully. Glass tinkled on to the ground. She looked around inside the car. No one was moving. She leaned back and felt Mutt's pulse. He was alive. She half stood up and duck-walked to the front of the limo. She bent over the front seat to see if Jeff was alive or dead. His eyes were closed. She felt his pulse. Faint but alive. She gingerly extricated herself from the car.

When she was finally standing on the sidewalk and away from the car, she looked up and saw they had crashed in front of a women's dress shop. All the mannequins were dressed in black and white. Interesting, she thought.

She looked around. A crowd had gathered. She could see police cars and an ambulance. She wondered what was wrong with her. She should have called 911. Someone else must have. She felt weird and stupid. A policeman approached her.

"Were you in that limo?" he asked.

"Yes. I was in there against my will. The guy in the back seat grabbed me as I came out of the hospital. The guy in the front seat kept turning around and talking to the guy in the back seat and not watching where he was going. I think that's why we crashed. I had my eyes closed."

The officer showed Elle his badge and identified himself.

"I'm officer Larry Evans. How do you feel?"

Elle took a quick inventory of her anatomy. "I think I'm fine!"

Officer Evans frowned. "I'll take your statement and then I think you should go to the hospital and get checked out just to be safe. Are you sure you're feeling ok? I'm going to have an ambulance take you up there, but I need you to wait. Do you mind sitting in the police car for a few minutes until I can deal with these two men?" He took her name, address and phone number.

"I can't believe this is happening!" Elle felt the tears welling up.

Officer Evans took her arm and gently helped her into his police car. He and his partner then had the paramedics deal with the two unconscious men. They sent Jeff first. The next ambulance took Mutt.

Officer Evans came back to Elle in a few minutes and asked her how she was doing.

"I really feel ok," she said.

He thought for a minute. "We're still waiting on the next ambulance, so I'd like to take you up to the hospital myself and just have you looked at."

"I really feel fine, but I'm happy to cooperate." She shrugged.

"That's great," Officer Evans said. "I just don't like leaving you here standing on the sidewalk after an accident. Is there someone I can call for you?"

Elle chuckled. "No, I should make the call. You'll cause a heart attack."

The officer smiled. "So, if you don't mind, I'll take you up to the hospital and you can call someone after you've been seen." Elle shrugged again. Officer Evans shut the door. As she rode along, feeling like a criminal, she wondered about who had been in this back seat before her. Drunks, and criminals. None of them probably showered and shaved. Ewww, she thought.

Officer Evans walked her into the ER and talked to the receptionist. The receptionist gave her the usual clip board and a pen. "It's déjà vu all over again!" she quipped. Officer Evans looked at her, obviously puzzled. He and Elle found two seats together and he asked questions about what had happened. She told the story as well as she could. Thankfully she had already given him her name, address and phone. She wondered to herself if she shouldn't just order business cards so she wouldn't have to keep repeating her name and address every time she ended up in an altercation resulting in police presence.

Elle spent the rest of the afternoon in the ER, being watched for concussion. They insisted she have a brain scan, so she complied. She told them she felt fine, but they were being cautious.

Dr Bennett came in about five p.m. "How are you feeling?"

Elle smiled. "Actually, very well. How do YOU think I'm doing?"

He smiled back. "The scan came back negative, so I feel better about letting you leave, if you wish."

Elle was relieved. "Yes, I wish!"

"Ok," he said. "The girls will bring your paperwork."

She thanked him and he hurried away to his next patient.

The nurse brought in the paperwork, and she signed on the dotted lines.

"Do you have someone you can call?"

Elle told her yes. "My sister works here so I'm just going to go to her office and ask her to take me home."

The nurse said that would be fine. "Are you ok to walk or would you like a wheelchair?"

"No," Elle replied. "I feel fine. I can walk. Thank you so much."

She slung her purse over her shoulder and walked out of the ER. She stopped in the hallway to pull her phone out of her purse and call Mandy. Since it was after five, she may have already left. Mandy answered.

"Hi Sis, where are you?"

"I'm still at the office. Why?"

"Oh, good. Wait for me. I'll be there in a minute, and I'll explain."

"Oh! Are you ok? Ok! Ok. Tell me when you get here."

In a few minutes, Elle was standing in Mandy's office trying to hold back the tears so she could explain. She paced while she talked.

"When I left here earlier, I was grabbed by those goons that broke into George's office and might have killed Butch. I'm not sure about that last part."

"What?" Mandy gaped. "What are you talking about?"

"It was really crazy. One minute I was standing on the sidewalk hailing a cab and the next minute I was in the back of a limo with those stupid goons! It was ghastly. Those guys have never heard of a toothbrush or mouth wash! The guy driving was the one we call Jeff and the guy sitting beside me was the one we call Mutt. They were yelling at each other. Well Jeff was yelling at Mutt when he should have been watching the road. The next thing I know we're in a crumpled heap on the sidewalk."

Mandy was horrified. "My dear Lord in Heaven, what next?" She finished straightening up her desk, pulled her purse out of the bottom drawer and came around to where Elle was pacing. "Let's go. You're making a ridge in my carpet."

They walked together to the employee parking lot, located Mandy's BMW and climbed in. Elle leaned back in the seat, exhausted. Mandy drove unhurriedly to Elle's hotel. She pulled up in front and waited while Elle leaned over and kissed her cheek and then exited the car. She walked around to Mandy's side to talk to her. She rested her arm on the ledge of the open window and told her thanks again.

Mandy put her hand on Elle's arm. "Do you want me to come in with you?

Elle smiled. "No. I think I just want to go upstairs and lie down. Thanks again."

Mandy patted Elle's arm. "Any time, except not for this anymore, ok?"

Elle saluted. "I promise. I hope," she said. Mandy waited until Elle was in the lobby of the hotel before she drove away.

Back in her hotel room, Elle lay on her back diagonally across the freshly made bed and stared at the ceiling, "George, where are you?" she asked out loud. She tapped her temples with her fingertips. "Send me a message, George!"

She dozed.

She sat up and looked at the clock. Eight p.m. No messages from Agent Travis or George. She stood up, resolute.

"Elle," she said out loud, "This may be the stupidest thing you've ever done." She grabbed her purse and made tracks to her car. With new vigor she drove back to Macy's and made a bee line for the dress department. With the salesperson's help she found what she wanted: a simple but elegant black dress. Next stop, the jewelry department. Pearl earrings and a simple pearl necklace added to her purchases. Final stop, make up. Oh good. The girl at the Lancôme counter was doing demos. She dawdled around until it was her turn. She said to the girl, "Give me the works!" She was on a mission and the girl got to work. When she was finished, she showed Elle the mirror.

"Well! Hellooo, Gorgeous!" Elle smiled wearily.

The technician looked closely at her face one last time and admired her handiwork. "You are beautiful!"

Elle was reminded of what Butch would say when she took extra special care with her looks. 'Putting on the armor, are we?'

Next stop, the restroom. She walked in with her shopping bags and came out wearing the black dress and the jewelry. Her concourse shoes were in the car, and she was set. On her way to the exits many a male head spun on its axis and eyeballs fell out of their sockets. Elle wasn't paying attention.

Nerves taut, blood pumping, she parked close to the door in case she needed a fast get away. She switched from flip flops to her black patent pumps and marched determinedly toward Berlusconi.

Elle stepped inside and looked around. It was busy tonight. There must be a special, she thought. Steeling her nerves, she chose a seat at the bar. In a few moments, the bartender asked for her order. He studied her face. Elle wondered what was wrong. Did she have spinach in her teeth? Why did he keep staring at her?

"Do I know you?" she asked.

He frowned. "I don't think so… but I feel like I should know you."

"Actually," Elle smiled her best smile. "I was here with a friend a few days ago and we loved the food!"

"Oh, yes, Anton is Cordon Bleu trained. There's not a finer chef anywhere."

"Well, it certainly showed the other night. I couldn't wait to come back!"

"So, where is your friend tonight?"

"He couldn't get away. I was bored so I decided to take myself out."

"Hey that's great! An independent woman. What would you like to drink?"

"Oh, I don't know. Maybe I'll have my salad and my drink together tonight. How about humoring me with a Bloody Mary?"

When he brought her drink, he stood and talked to her for a while. Finally, it seemed to her like a lightbulb came on in his head. "You're Butch's girlfriend, aren't you? I've seen your picture, but he never brought you in here. I wonder why?"

"I've wondered that lately, myself. This is a beautiful establishment. It seems like he'd have wanted me to see it. I was on cloud nine the other night. The décor is tasteful, the food is out of this world. The staff is gracious. No one could fault it for anything."

"Well, he probably didn't want to mix business with pleasure, right?" He seemed to think what he said was clever. and moved down the bar to wait on a newcomer.

Elle nearly choked. She swallowed carefully and wondered if the bartender knew the significance of what he had just said. Should she play dumb? Or should she act like she knew it all the time? Gahh! What a dilemma! If she acted like she already knew everything that might encourage him to talk. That would be good. But acting like she didn't know anything could save her life... Hmmm... Well, she came here tonight to get some information so she might as well get as much as she can or die trying. She winced at that. Too true to be funny!

The bartender came back to visit with her again. She looked at his name tag. It said "Vince."

"Well, Vince, I guess I just didn't measure up. I'm not as pretty as the other girls so he left me home." She tried to look sad.

"Are you kidding? You are the best looking of any of them! I think he was keeping you back for himself! You could have made a fortune in here!"

"Oh, Vince, you're just trying to make me feel better! It's ok. We all know our limitations. You don't have to lie to make me feel better! But you are so sweet!"

Elle slid out of the easy chair. "I think I'll have dinner now. Could you get the hostess to find me a table? I keep thinking about that Sfogliatella!"

Vince snapped his fingers and motioned for the hostess. She came over to Elle and told her it would be just a minute. Elle asked for a booth rather than a table. The hostess whose name tag said "Carla" said that would be fine. Elle finished her Bloody Mary and ate the olive she had saved for last. She swiveled in her chair waiting to be called and absently looked at the line of people at the bar, all sitting in the overstuffed chairs instead of the usual bar stools. She liked these chairs so much better. Being short, it was hard to hoist up onto some of the really high stools.

Carla came to get her and led her to a booth. Happily for Elle, it was near the fireplace where there was a cheery crackling fire. She told Carla she was going to the restroom and would be right back. Laying the menu down, Carla smiled and went to get water and silverware.

Elle casually strolled down the hall following the signs. In the restroom she looked around, washed her hands, looked in the mirror and told her face to get a grip. Things were going ok. She yanked the paper towel out of the dispenser and held it mid-air. Paper Towel. Paper towel dispenser? Paper towel. Really? She grimaced and quickly examined the dispenser closely. It was tightly attached to the wall. She felt around inside and underneath. Nothing. Well, what did she expect? It was a bit arcane and kind of silly. And yet... She stuck her head out of the restroom door and looked up and down the hall. No one.

She popped out and hurriedly tiptoed to the men's restroom. She opened the door a crack. She couldn't see anyone. Her heart pounding, she slipped in and shut the door with her eye already on the paper towel dispenser. She tiptoed over and felt all around the front, sides, underneath and the top. She peered closely where the dispenser attached to the wall. She felt all around the seam. Same thing on the other side. She felt along the seam. There was a tiny lump. She eyed the lump. Something white. Like whoever was cleaning, got a piece of rag caught. She used her fingernail to try to get a hold of it. It moved and she pulled on it more. Out came an envelope. She was trembling.

She strained to hear if anyone was coming. She held on to the envelope and ran, still on her tiptoes, towards one of the stalls. She looked up and chose one that had most of the light from the ceiling. She closed the door and locked it. With unsteady hands she carefully opened the envelope and pulled out a piece of paper. There was a lot of writing. She pulled her phone out of her bra and took several pictures. She put the paper back in the envelope and took a picture of it and then snuck out and put it back. She took a picture of the dispenser and the crack where just white showed. She shoved it in as far as she could.

Phone back in her bra, she peeked out. Amazingly, there was no one. She tiptoed back to the women's restroom and slipped back inside. She was sweating. She checked her hair and then casually opened the door and walked normally, with her high heels clicking on the tile floor, back to her table.

She slid into the booth, breathed a sigh of relief, and fanned herself with her menu.

"Are you thinking of changing gender, Elle?" a man's voice asked her.

She visibly jumped, losing control of her menu, which flew across the table.

Agent Carson appeared in her line of sight. "May I join you?"

Chapter 27

Elle was flabbergasted.

Dan stood at her table waiting for her to say something. As usual he was dressed to impress. Brioni navy suit, Brioni pale blue dress shirt and tie. Of course, the proverbial Rolex loaded with diamonds, she thought sarcastically. What on God's green earth was he doing to make enough money for this bling wardrobe?

When she could finally speak, she said, "No! What are YOU doing here?

Dan looked put out. "Come on, Elle, all is forgiven. Have a heart!"

"You're forgiving ME? That's rich." Elle glared at him.

"I saw you come out of the men's restroom. What were you doing in there?"

They stared at each other. Elle wondered again if she should play it straight or play dumb. But she was pretty sure he knew she had picked up a lot of information since their last encounter. She decided to start out being nice.

"Oh, alright. Please sit down and join me!"

Dan slid into the opposite side of the booth, handed back her prodigal menu, and crossed his arms on the table. "So? What were you doing in the men's restroom?"

"Oh, I like to see if the men's restrooms are as nice as the ladies.' It's a thing I have. I check out all the restrooms – especially in the nice places. I'm sorry I kicked you. You don't seem to be walking with a limp."

"No thanks to you, but" he smiled sweetly, "I don't hold grudges. So, no hard feelings?"

This was kind of stupid, Elle thought. But she decided to play along for a while. "Of course not, it's very kind of you. You have a beautiful place here. And Vince tells me you snagged a Cordon Bleu chef. How ever did you manage that?"

Elle's brain was on whizz cycle. Dan didn't blink an eye when she called the restaurant his. Either he didn't hear her, or she was spot on. He was the BIG BOSS!

Just then, Dan raised his hand, snapped his fingers, displaying a big fat diamond ring, and a server instantly appeared like Rosey the Robot waiting on George Jetson. He looked at Elle.

"Drink? Appetizer?"

Why not, she thought. "Could I have a Margarita, blended, please? And salt please."

Dan ordered a martini and the server disappeared.

He continued explaining how he was able to snag a great chef. "Well, his dad owed me a favor, so he offered his son to work for me. It's the best thing that could have happened! Since he's been here, we're packed every night. Business is great."

"Well, I wish you many years of success and everything you deserve!"

Dan frowned. "What does THAT mean?"

"Nothing! I mean you've worked really hard to get what you want. So, you should get all that you deserve."

"I'm not sure I like the sound of that."

"Well," she said quietly, "if you know anything at all about George and his whereabouts and you don't take me to him at once I'll see you get exactly what you deserve."

Elle's eyes were steely blue, and they bore into Dan's soul.

Dan shook it off and stood up. "Would you like to come with me?"

"Where?"

"To see George, of course."

"You're lying."

"Come see for yourself."

She reluctantly slid out of the booth and stood up. Thinking she was going to her death, she followed him down the hall. As she walked behind Dan, she could hear voices and sexual noises behind some of the doors. She grimaced. She was immensely grossed out, and she was sure she was going to need a shower if she ever made it back to the hotel.

They finally stopped at one of the doors. Dan brought a key from his suit breast pocket and unlocked the door. Elle followed him into the room.

George was sitting in a chair in just his hospital gown. He had ropes around his feet and arms, a gag in his mouth, and blood seeping out of a wound over his right eye. He was going to have one royal shiner. There were blood stains on his thigh where his wound was. He looked half asleep, like he'd been drugged. His left eye opened wide when he saw Elle.

Elle burst into tears. She ran to him and put her arms around him. He was cold to the touch. She held him and sobbed. Then she whirled around and yelled at Dan. "You beat him up? A wounded hospital patient? You felt the need to hurt him more? Did this make you feel big and tough to hurt a man who can't fight back? And he's freezing cold! You couldn't bother to offer him a blanket? What is the matter with you? Have you no heart at all for any human? You are inhuman slime!" she screamed. Days of extreme stress, heartache, misery, guilt, physical trauma and fury all rose up into seething rage and with all the strength she could muster, she slapped Dan hard across the face.

Dan yelled in pain and grabbed Elle's arm. "First of all, shut up! You'll have everyone in the restaurant wondering what's going on! So, shut up!"

Mutt and Jeff were standing in the doorway. Elle looked at them. They didn't seem to be seriously injured. Jeff had a band-aid on his forehead. They had heard the yelling. Dan turned to them and told them with clenched teeth to get a blanket for the prisoner. "And some rope!" he called after them.

Dan pushed Elle into a chair. "Sit down and stay there!"

Elle was sure she had crossed the line. She was trembling. She knew that at this moment her life had become disposable, but she couldn't remember ever being this angry. Her teeth were chattering. She told herself to shut up and not say anything more, but as usual she wasn't listening. She was too angry. "We know all about you, you know. If you kill us both you're still not going to get away with it. You've got a sheet a mile long and they all know it." Elle's teeth were chattering. She was freezing and sweating. Why couldn't she just shut up?

"Sheet? Well, look at you and all your gangster talk."

She couldn't stop. She was frightened and furious. "Yes, we know your bartender paid Butch in weed and cash for bringing in girls to hook for you. Oh, don't look so surprised. Yes, we know you have hookers in all these rooms back here! When I first met you, I thought you were a class act, but how wrong I was. You're just a low life, a bottom feeder. We know you hired Alonzo to kill Butch. And we know Alonzo shot George and we know that bullet was meant for me. And we know Alonzo stole Butch's car. And your hapless lackeys Tony and Franco – we call them Mutt and Jeff—can't get anything right. I don't know why you keep them on your payroll. I wonder about the arrangement you have with your Chef's father. It sounds pretty fishy to me." Why couldn't she shut up?

"Well, listen to you! Aren't you so smart? You don't know everything. There are things yet to be uncovered, and it might not be good for your health to know these things."

"Well, you're going to kill us anyway, why not entertain us?" Elle watched him. He was visibly puffing up before their eyes. She had discovered his Achilles heel. He wasn't getting the attention he wanted working for the FBI and he needed to do things that impress his superiors. Elle wondered where and when he had gone off the rails. Thomas Carlyle was right, she thought. 'Egotism is the source and summary of all faults and miseries.'

Mutt and Jeff brought the rope and wrapped George in the blanket. They tied the rope around Elle's ankles and arms.

She watched Dan strut. "It was me," he said. I planned it. I arranged it. I hired Butch to do my clean up. I just couldn't get my hands dirty. Have you ever heard of Danny the Don?"

Elle shook her head.

"Well, at this most historic moment you have the privilege of seeing Danny the Don in the flesh. That's me. I'm THE BOSS. And Alonzo is my Consigliere. Hah! You didn't know! I've worked for the FBI for ten years and no one knew what we were really doing! Such fools! Those stupid idiots at the FBI didn't know I helped them! Agents would arrest these criminals and their shady lawyers would get them off! All that detective work just down the drain. They'd make deals and go into witness protection! I had a hell of a hard time finding some of them. Don't you see? I've been helping the FBI all these years like the Good Samaritan!" Danny the Don chortled maniacally. He was not the same Dan Elle and George first met. Something had gone terribly wrong inside Dan's head.

Elle was speechless, for the moment. She looked around the room. Mutt and Jeff were behind Dan waiting for instructions. They seemed a little shocked at all this weird confession. She looked at George. His eyes were as big as saucers--well, the undamaged eye was. The other one was still half shut.

Elle managed to say, "What is it you do that helps the FBI? What do you mean Butch was your clean up man?"

Dan chortled. "You won't like it. He was the one –"

BOOM!

His sentence was cut short by a deafening explosion. Dust and chunks of plaster fell from the ceiling. Smoke billowed into the room from the hallway and through the vents. Elle coughed. She looked over at George. He started coughing, which made her thankful he was alive, but if they didn't get away from this smoke he was going to be in worse trouble. She wondered if she could bounce her chair around so she could untie him, but he was so groggy she wasn't sure he'd be able to reciprocate.

She heard voices. Doors opening. Women's voices. Screaming. Yelling "Shut the door!" Doors slamming shut. Again. More doors opening and slamming shut. More screaming. She was grossed out at the thought of all those FBI agents breaking in on those hookers and their customers. Then Agent Travis burst into the room followed by several police, uniforms and plain clothes, as well as paramedics with stretchers.

Someone was untying George, giving him oxygen, and carefully lifting him onto the stretcher. Ambulance people took him away.

Agent Travis was untying her. "Are you ok?"

"Yes," Elle said, "just a bit wheezy."

Agent Travis had one of the paramedics give her some oxygen. Then he directed them to put Elle on a stretcher and take her too, just to be safe.

"No, I don't want to!" Elle pulled away.

"Yes, you need to get checked out. I'll come and see you when I'm done here."

"Agent Travis!" She grabbed his arm. "They're all here!" The paramedics were lifting her onto the stretcher. They uncurled her fingers from the material on Agent Travis's jacket and gently pushed her flat on the stretcher. She popped back up again. "Dan is in the building and so are Mutt and Jeff!" Once again, the paramedic made her lie flat as he tightened the straps. They were taking her out into the hallway. She got louder. "I think the bartender is in it too. Also, check out the chef. I think he's some kind of payment for a job!" Agent Travis could still hear her voice echoing down the hall, and he could hear the Paramedic say, "Please, Miss, leave the mask on your face." The agent was shaking his head.

When they arrived at the Emergency Room, Dr Bennett was waiting for George. They took both George and Elle back to the treatment area where they were thoroughly examined and treated for smoke inhalation. They kept Elle on oxygen while they treated George. The surgeon removed the bandages on George's wound, pleased to see it seemed to be healing in spite of the filthy bandages, all that thrashing around, and the rest of his body being treated so badly. They treated all his abrasions and contusions, put them both in wheelchairs then sent both him and Elle back up to his room.

The nursing staff had arranged for them to be in George's room together. The rest of the night, staff popped in to say hello and welcome back.

Hillary and Jeannie both stopped in to see them. George asked them if there was a possibility of food. "I missed dinner."

Elle and the nurses laughed. Elle told them he was insistent there was nothing wrong with his stomach. His leg was injured not his stomach.

Pretty soon here came Hillary with a tray of cheese, crackers, sodas and cookies. George beamed. Elle was hoping he'd share.

Hospital staff continued to drop in to say welcome back. George slept, or attempted to sleep between drop ins, so they didn't have any time to talk but Elle was content to just be there in the bed next to his, knowing he was safe.

They slept all night. Elle didn't even stir when they came in to check George's vitals.

Chapter 28

Elle woke on Wednesday morning wondering where she was. Memory arrived. She looked over to see George sleeping peacefully in the hospital bed. After the last few days, she was positively glowing with relief. She whispered, "Thank you so much, dear Lord!" She stretched luxuriously while lazily thinking about what she might do today. She could go home! A sobering thought, but a satisfying one. She was anxious to see how bad the house looked after being ransacked more than once.

When she could see George was awake, she slid out of her bed and crept over to him. He reached out and brought her close to him and they hugged. They hugged with relief and thanks they both were safe. Elle stepped back to reach for the button to raise the head of his bed. She could hear activity in the hallway and knew breakfast was being delivered, so she pulled the tray table into position for George. The kitchen had used George's standing order which was fine with them. Hot coffee never felt so good going down. Even hospital coffee was pretty good this morning!

While they were eating, the hospital administrator dropped in to apologize to George for their lack of security and told him they had never had anything like this happen before! George assured him they didn't blame the hospital and they were both very grateful for the care they were getting, before the abduction, and since. The administrator assured them security had been tightened in all areas of the hospital so this would never happen again. He also shared with them they had set up a memorial for the officer who was killed guarding George's room. There will be a commemorative memorial plaque on the wall at the end of the hallway. Also, the hospital will be paying for funeral expenses.

As the administrator was leaving, flowers arrived for both Elle and George. The card said, "With deep apologies. Our best to you as you recover." The signature was "The Hospital Staff." Elle called the hotel to find out if her room was available for tonight and was told yes. The desk agent reminded her she had extended her stay through the weekend so not to worry. She let them know she'd be in later. She called Mandy and Linda and filled them in.

George and Elle looked at each other. She said, "How do you feel? Please, not with your fingers."

He grinned. She felt like that was a good sign. "Like I've been pulled through a knot-hole backwards."

She smiled. "Well, that's encouraging!"

"Can't keep a good man down!"

"Nope, you sure can't."

Agent Travis strode in as if he had something to say. Elle offered him a chair. George told him how grateful he was for saving them both.

"Well," I appreciate the accolades, but it's I who owe you a debt."

They both looked surprised.

"Well, I had a lot of suppositions and theories. But when this crazy girl took it upon herself to walk into Berlusconi unarmed and alone, and managed not to get killed, she did us a huge favor! By the way, young lady, that was not very wise." He looked at Elle. Elle looked properly chastised. "I know. It was stupid, but I've never been known as the smart one." She grinned. "I probably need a keeper."

Agent Travis smiled. "The good news is, because of you, we finally had probable cause to get a search warrant. And that is huge."

"Oh! I just remembered!" Elle pulled her phone out of her bra and opened up her pictures. "Remember when the note in the black book said paper towel? I checked both restrooms, looked at the paper towel dispensers and I found this behind the one in the men's restroom."

Agent Travis scrolled through the pictures. "This is huge! This is remarkable! This is outstanding!"

"So, what does it mean?" Elle was puzzled.

"Before I tell you about Butch. I want to let you know we have the men you call "Mutt and Jeff" as well as Vince and Danny in custody. We took the chef in for questioning, thanks to Elle, and we found out the chef's father is former mafia who is in hiding because he chose to get out and go straight when his son was born." We've arranged to transport him home to Italy if he wishes.

He paused and yawned. "Sorry. I was going to say Bruce Mou, former head of the FBI's Gambino squad said a long time ago: 'You never leave the mob. Sometimes you're wishing you'd never gotten into it, when there's a contract on your life or you're going to jail. But you never leave. Death is the penalty for breaking any of the Mafia code, particularly omerta.'

Elle gave him a blank look. "Omerta?"
"Omerta is the code of honor that basically is the unbreakable rule. You don't ever talk to authorities, or outsiders. You don't cooperate with the authorities or outsiders, or the government, especially during a criminal investigation. You also don't interfere with the illegal activities of others. And you never contact the authorities or the government about any illegal activities.

Elle said, "So the code is to turn a blind eye to anything illegal and to never talk to anyone about anything."

"That pretty much sums it up," Agent Travis agreed.

Hillary came in to check on George. Elle asked the agent if he'd like coffee. He said no. He was hoping to go home to bed pretty soon, but he'd love some water. Hillary immediately went and got a fresh carafe of water and a glass and brought it back.

Agent Travis yawned again. "Sorry, I've been up for a week. Well 72 hours, I think." He looked at his notes. "We've learned a lot about Butch. First of all, his real name is Marco Colacurcio. His grandfather is Frank Colacurcio , Jr. In the 1950s, Frank Colacurcio, Sr. began operating cigarette and jukebox vending machines in the Seattle area. The vending machine businesses became important to organized crime figures who easily skimmed money.

Elle was obviously shocked. "What did you say? Butch was actually someone else? He'd been pretending to be someone that didn't exist?"

Agent Travis looked at Elle sympathetically. "I'm sorry. I'm sure this is hard for you."

Elle sighed. "Well, it explains a lot about his behavior, like trying to stay in character! But, sorry, please continue with this amazing history lesson!"

Agent Travis smiled. "In 1957, Colacurcio began working with Portland crime figure James "Big Jim" Elkins to open prostitution houses in Portland. In the 1960s, Colacurcio opened topless clubs in Seattle and skimmed money. In the 1970s, Colacurcio met with Bonanno crime family member Salvatore "Bill" Bonanno in Yakima, Washington to discuss a business relationship. When questioned about the meeting, Frank Colacurcio replied with "I went to Yakima to pick hot peppers, but I didn't pick no bananas."

Elle commented. "I know this is all terrible, but I thought that was funny."

Agent Travis looked at Elle and George. "I think it's healthy to find humor in all of this. It's definitely one for the books!" He continued. "In the following years Colacurcio continued to expand his strip club business. In 2003, a criminal investigation known as "Strippergate" began in Seattle, focusing on strip clubs owned by Frank Colacurcio, Sr. and his son, Frank Colacurcio Jr. In 2008, local police and federal agents raided Colacurcio's home and business. The strip clubs owned by Colacurcio were being used as fronts for brothels. In 2009, Colacurcio Sr., his son Frank Colacurcio

Jr. and four others were indicted and charged with conspiracy and racketeering. On July 2, 2010, boss Frank Colacurcio, Sr. died at the age of 93."

"No wonder Butch or Marco or whatever his name was, wouldn't talk about his family!" George commented.

Agent Travis agreed. "That is for sure. If he'd have slipped up, I wonder what might have happened to Elle. Thankfully, we don't have to worry about that." He stopped and poured himself a glass of water and took a drink. "Oh, that's good on the dry throat."

He looked at his notes. "Now about Vince, the bartender. He recruited Butch/Marco to snag girls to be hookers for Danny. Most of the girls that work at Berlusconi were recruited by Butch. Vince gave Butch weed as payment plus cash. As Danny got more comfortable with Butch, he gave him more jobs to do. That's when the business with the Black book started. That was Butch's first mistake. He wrote too much in the book.

"First?" Elle was indignant. "He made a lot of mistakes before that one!"

Agent Travis laughed. "He kept a written record of his assignments which he never should have done. And worse, he put the restaurant's address in the front cover and even wrote down the secret word to help him remember where to pick up his assignments. That was his second mistake. Leaving it under the bed at home was his third," he looked at Elle, "or some number down the list of mistakes. By the way, that was a lulu!"

Elle was frowning. "But I still don't see what you're talking about. What assignments?"

George's voice was gentle. "Elle, come over and sit with me."

Elle sighed and went over and sat with George on his bed. George put his arm around her. Then he nodded to Agent Travis. "OK, Arnie. Go."

Agent Travis' voice was gentle as well. "Elle, Butch was in a lot of trouble. He was addicted to gambling."

Elle interjected, "I knew that. He tried to hide it, but I knew."

"Well," Agent Travis continued. "He was in really deep. He owed money everywhere. He had been banned from all Las Vegas casinos. He owed several loan sharks. We've been watching him because of his ties with the Mafia, but also because he was working for Dan Carson. As you know, Dan is a dirty FBI agent, who is actually the owner of Berlusconi, which is a front for a prostitution ring. They have a state-of-the-art printing press for counterfeiting set up in the basement of the restaurant. The $20,000 you found was counterfeit, and that's why Butch got killed. He tried to pay his debts with counterfeit money."

Elle was speechless.

George finally said, "What about the black book?" Agent Travis sighed. "In that black book were the names of people who owed money to the loan sharks. It was Butch's job to warn people if they weren't paying. He went first to visit these individuals and if they didn't pay, then Franco and Tony would go and do damage. Butch was becoming unreliable, and they couldn't trust him. He kept disappearing. Usually off looking for someplace to gamble. Franco and Tony were getting mad. Butch lost the book, and they were desperate to get it back. They couldn't trust him to hang on to the book, so they started giving him the assignments one at a time. They had some sort of arrangement where he was supposed to go to the restaurant and pick up his next assignment." Elle and George both nodded.

Elle finally said, "He sure was a busy boy. Between picking up girls for Vince and leaning on the poor people who owed money, you'd think he'd be able to pay his debts."

Agent Travis gave Elle a sympathetic look. "He was way into debt before he even started working for Danny. He was never going to be able to pay it off. It might make you feel better he refused to kill anyone. They would have paid him a lot of money to do a hit for them. But he seemed to draw the line at murder."

George shook his head. "I cannot believe we're talking so casually about Elle's ex, counterfeit money, and murder! It boggles the mind."

"By the way, Elle," interjected Agent Travis. "The money Butch gave you to repair your wall was counterfeit, so don't try to spend it."

Elle and George looked at each other and rolled their eyes. They both laughed.

George said, "The tip we left at Berlusconi the other night was part of that cash. Ooops! By the way, what did Carson mean when he was bragging about helping the FBI like a Good Samaritan?"

Agent Travis looked disgusted. "I think Carson was burned out. He was stressed and angry because, as always in law enforcement, sometimes the people you try to put behind bars end up lawyering up and getting off. I think he was starting to let it get to him, and he started murdering the ones he felt were guilty but let go. He started believing he was doing a good deed by killing criminals."

Elle had one more question for Agent Travis. "What was the explosion in Berlusconi?"

The Agent grinned. "That was our back up. We wanted to take everyone alive and there was the possibility of a gunfight. So we decided on a distraction. We quietly arrested all the kitchen help first and then we just blew up the kitchen!

During this last sentence, Mandy and Linda walked in.

They both stopped in the doorway.

Mandy said, "Whose kitchen got blown up?"

George and Elle grinned.

Elle said, "Come in! We'll explain!"

Chapter 29

Dr Bennett walked in and looked around the room, his eyes resting on Agent Travis. "Am I interrupting?"

Agent Travis jumped up. "Absolutely not. George and Elle, I'll keep you posted." He gave the surgeon a slight salute and left the room.

Elle stood up and gathered up some chairs for Mandy and Linda. They sat and listened to the surgeon talk to George.

"Well, young man, you've been through the war! How do you feel?"

Elle caught George's eye. She shook her pointer finger at him, warning him not to say, "with my fingers."

George grinned. "It's been entertaining, to say the least! Dr Bennett looked through his half glasses down at the chart. "It seems, in spite of everything, if you'd like to go home today, you can!"

George smiled. "That is great news!"

Elle was delighted.

The surgeon lifted the sheet away from George's leg. "Let's take a look."

Linda put her hands over her eyes.

Dr Bennett peeled the bandages away and peered closely at the wound, sniffing, and pressing gently around the edges, checking for swelling, heat, and oozing. "What's your pain level today?" he asked George. "Does this hurt?" He pressed while watching George's face.

George winced, but he said, "A little, but not bad."

Dr Bennett was impressed with the progress. "It's healing nicely. He patted George's shoulder and motioned for the nurse to step in and put on the fresh bandage.

"I'm including a prescription for some pain medicine just in case. You can fill it or not. The nurse will give it to you along with your discharge papers and your next post-op appointment. So, I'll see you in two weeks, unless something happens, and I need to see you sooner. Oh, and there are orders for physical therapy too."

He stopped to look at Elle. "Are you ok, young lady? You had quite a scare yesterday. The nurse has discharge papers for you too."

Elle smiled. "Yes, thank you. And thanks for everything you've done for George."

He patted her on the shoulder and disappeared into the hall. The nurse finished up with the fresh bandages and then explained about the papers she was having him sign: One with wound care instructions, one with general discharge instructions with his appointment date, and one to sign that said he understood all the instructions. She asked him if he wanted some help dressing and he said he didn't think so since there seemed to be quite a bit of available help in the room.

Elle had bought him some basketball shorts to wear home, since she didn't think jeans would fit over the bandages. She had also brought socks and a t-shirt since the clothes he had been wearing were bloody and had been cut off when they were prepping him for surgery. She carefully helped him sit up on the edge of the bed and got his feet into the right pant legs, put his new socks on and his shoes and then helped him stand up.

"Are you ok?" she asked. "Feel lightheaded or dizzy?"

George thought a minute. "No. I feel ok."

She helped him get his pants all the way up and then she let him get his shirt on. When she had finished with George, the nurse had her do her paperwork. Then she looked at both of them and told them to be careful and stay safe, and she'd be back to take them down to the lobby.

Elle looked down at herself and scowled. "I look like a hag. I've slept in my clothes so much lately I feel like a homeless person."

Mandy spoke up. "Hey Elle, you never finished telling me about the brain scan."

There was a chorus of "What?" around the room.

Elle looked around. "I guess I never got a chance to tell you guys what happened. Well, I came to the hospital to have coffee with Mandy and when I left, Mutt and Jeff grabbed me and threw me in the back of the limo. But they started arguing and Jeff kept looking back at Mutt and ran us into a telephone pole, I think. I never saw what we hit. Anyway, the officer brought me up here and made me have a brain scan to make sure I was ok."

Mandy laughed. "Did they find one?"

Elle laughed too. "Very funny. Well, I suppose they didn't. They said it was negative. That means minus, right?"

They were both laughing. Linda and George were grinning.

Mandy said, "Well, you know what Mom always says to you when you say you're going to give someone a piece of your mind. 'Can you afford it?'"

That made them all laugh more.

Mandy got serious. "Are you sure you're ok?"

"Oh yes, I'm f-f-f-fine." Elle looked at her sister and showed her an exaggerated twitch in her left eye. "But I forgot to tell you when we crashed in the limo, we landed in front of a really cool dress shop. Just looking in the windows it seems all they sell is black and white clothing! Isn't that wild?"

Linda said, "Wow, just your cup of tea!"

The nurse arrived back to take them down to the front door. Elle told her they were leaving the flowers for her to share with another patient.

Linda and Mandy discussed who would take them to their hotel. Linda volunteered. So, Mandy asked the nurse if she needed help pushing wheelchairs. The nurse said it would be appreciated. So Mandy pushed Elle, the nurse pushed George. Linda went on ahead to get the car. Out on the sidewalk Mandy hugged George and kissed Elle and said she'd see them soon. She took Elle's wheelchair and went back inside to drop off the chair and return to her office.

Linda was in the patient pickup lane when they all arrived downstairs to the lobby. The nurse was pushing George holding a bag of cards and gifts in the wheelchair and Elle was in charge of the large stuffed dog, courtesy of nephew, Georgie.

The nurse got them all tucked into the car and returned to her duties.

Linda looked at George in the front seat beside her. "Are you ok? You look a bit worn out."

"I'm ok. It was a lot of work getting dressed and discharged and getting in the car. I'm weak and out of shape!"

Linda frowned. "Well, naturally! Your body has taken quite a beating! You need rest and recouperation! Where would you like to go?

Elle leaned forward from her spot in the back seat. "We have a couple more days in the hotel. Why don't we go there for at least one more night before we tackle our homes? What do you think, Lin?"

"That's a good idea," Linda agreed. "You can go there and regroup and make some plans."

Linda pulled up in front of the hotel and told the doorman she'd be right back. She helped George out of the car while Elle gathered up belongings and they walked into the hotel that had become their second home.

The concierge met them and offered them a wheelchair.

Elle beamed. "How wonderful! Thank you!"

The concierge beamed right back and said it was his pleasure and would they like him to assist them to their room?

Elle thanked him and turned to Linda. "You're out of a job, but do you want to come up?"

Linda smiled. "No, you go ahead. Looks like George is in good hands! We'll talk later about lunch, ok?"

Elle hugged her. "Yes, lunch please. So nice to almost be normal!"

They waved good-bye and Elle hurried to catch the elevator.

Finally, up in their hide-away, the concierge helped get George stretched out on his bed. Elle fluffed the pillows and made sure he was comfortable. She thanked the concierge and handed him a large tip. He smiled and quietly closed the door behind him.

Elle flopped back on her bed and studied the ceiling. Relief. Shock and awe at everything that had transpired. A wistfulness at the surprise about Butch and how he was nothing like she thought. She looked over at George. His eyes were closed. She decided to order some room service.

She picked up the phone. "Hi! I'd like to order a chicken Caesar salad."

A voice from the next bed interjected, "And a cheeseburger with everything."

"You just got out of the hospital," she whispered. Don't you want soup or something?"

"There is nothing wrong with my stomach. It was my leg that was injured. Cheeseburger please?"

Elle snickered and removed her hand from over the mouthpiece. "I'm so sorry about that. Please add a cheeseburger with everything and fries as well."

"Dessert please" came the voice behind her.

"And also, dessert, please? Pie or cake or cheesecake? Uh…"

"Cheesecake" came the voice.

"Two cheesecakes please. Thank you so much!"

Elle looked over at George. His eyes were closed, but he was smiling.

"Goofball." She said.

She lay back against the pillows and just let her mind flow. She thought about everything that had happened, and in spite of some of it, she felt blessed they both had been spared their lives.

Eventually, there was a knock at the door. Her heart did a flip flop and she went to the door and opened it a crack. A uniformed waiter. With food. Good.

She opened the door and let him in. She told him to just set the tray on the bed. He did and she handed him some bills. She let him out and then locked the door.

She looked over at George. He was carefully scooting up so his back was against the pillows. She moved the tray of food over to his bed and went around and sat by him.

"Can you see if the Mariners are playing?" he asked her.

She got up and looked for the remote and brought it to him and regained her place beside him.

Look at this! My two favorite things in all the world – the remote and you!"

Elle rolled her eyes.

"You know what I've told you about that."

Elle laughed. "Yeah yeah. Blabbity blah. Yes. Stuck blah blah in the back of my head. Blah."

George held the remote in his left hand, put his right arm around Elle and pulled her close to him. "You know I like you better than the remote. You don't have to worry about competition." He looked into her eyes and then his lips came down gently on hers. All the love he had felt for her for all the years, was fervently and shamelessly wired into that kiss. There was relief, gratitude, and passion in that kiss. Elle read the message loud and clear. Everything she had felt, the resistance, the worry, the hesitance, all flew away. Arms were wrapped tight and emotions on high after the terrible week they both had suffered. Personal energy flowed back and forth until it was fused into one power source. She could hear her heart beating in her ears.

A phone ringing shocked them apart.

George said, "That's me." He scrabbled around and finally found it in his back pocket. "Hey, hi Linda! Yes! We're good. We ordered up some lunch and we're just going to laze around. Yes, I have an appointment in two weeks. Yes, I think we'll check out tomorrow and go take a look at Elle's house. We've heard it's in bad shape. It sounds like it might be uninhabitable. Yes, they told Elle my house was tossed but there is no structural damage, thankfully. So, Elle will come stay with me for a while. We don't know. Sure! Yes. I promise! Yes, I'm telling you the truth. I really am ok. No. I promise. I won't overdo. OK, sis! Thanks!"

Elle started in on her salad.

George felt around for the remote and searched until he found a game. Low and behold, Mariners! It was a sixth sense, she was sure.

They sat companionably side by side, watched the game and ate their lunch.

In a while, she asked him what the plans were.

George, his eyes on the game, said, "Get your rig, check your house, probably hire a contractor to repair the structural damage, then hire a cleaning company to clean your house, go down and sign statements, and..."

Elle waited. In a minute she said, "And?"

George continued, his eyes still on the game, "Check my house to make sure it's livable, hire cleaners just because if you're going to stay with me, it should get a thorough cleaning, ...

Elle waited to see if there was anything else. In a minute she said again, "And?"

George smiled, still facing the television, "Hire cleaners for the office; I think I can get the interns to help me with straightening up the files... check in with Linda to see if there is anything critical, and ..."

Elle sighed. "And?"

George looked at her and grinned. He leaned over and kissed her. "It's bottom of the ninth, bases are loaded, two outs, full count, down by a run."

She flicked him in the head.

He looked at her and rolled his eyes.

She laughed out loud.

She leaned back in the curve of his body with his arm around her and felt blessed. She loved this man so much. He had been through so much for her, all the while catering to her. She did not deserve him, but she wanted him terribly. She did not want to lose him.

Chapter 30

One year later…

     It was lunch time. Elle was in a booth at the Thirsty Lion.
Bobbi, Elle and George's favorite server appeared. "Hi, Elle! It's
been ages! How are you? Can I bring you something to drink?"

     "Hi Bobbi! I know. It's been too long! Yes, diet Pepsi,
please?"

     George arrived and slid in across from Elle. He grinned at
Bobbi. "Hi Bobbi! Nice to see you! Pepsi for me too, thanks!"

     Bobbi left to fill the order.

     George faced Elle. He was smiling from ear to ear. "I've got
great news!"

     Elle grinned back. "So do I, but you go first."

     "Are you sure? I'm happy for you to go first. I'm a
gentleman, ladies first." George was still grinning.

     Elle smiled. "It's ok, you first."

     George put his hand out across the table and covered her
hand with his. "So, Agent Travis called me today. The trial is over.
Danny and Alonzo both got life in prison. Mutt and Jeff each got
twenty years and Vince got ten. And because you helped bring them
down, you get the $20,000 reward!

     Elle was thrilled. "That is fabulous!"

     George squeezed her hand. "OK, now what's your news?"

     George repeated. "What's your news?"

     Elle looked serious. "I went to the doctor today."

     George frowned. "Oh no. What's the matter? Are you ok?"

     Elle smiled. "How would you feel about being a daddy?"

     George's mouth fell open. He blinked. He blinked again.
He reached for a napkin.

     "Are you crying?"

George sniffed and wiped his eyes. "No, I must have allergies." He reached across the table with both hands and took hers. A little tear escaped and rolled down his cheek unheeded. "Have I told you how much I love you?"

"Every time you look at me, my darling." Elle was tearing up.

Bobbie arrived with the sodas. He thanked her and she asked if they wanted to order. "Give us about ten minutes," George said to her. She smiled, nodded and disappeared.

"I've an idea." Elle looked seriously across at George. "What if we use that $20,000 to start a fund or a foundation or a trust or something to help all your pro bono clients get back on their feet and steer them in a better direction? What do you think? We got that money because of a lot of criminal activity so this is kind of a way to counteract that. Is that silly?"

George wiped his eyes again with his tattered napkin. "Darn allergies." Reaching across the table he said, "I didn't think I could possibly love you more, but I do."

It was Elle's turn to wipe her eyes on her napkin. George raised his soda. "To my beautiful wife, Elle, whom I thank every day for proposing to me!"

Beaming, she raised her soda. "To my handsome husband, George, who, thankfully, never gave up on me!"

They clinked glasses. "To the King!"

Italian Sfogliatelle Recipe

Now that you have some idea what a sfogliatella is, the next step, of course, is to know how to make them. Here's an easy recipe to help you with that.

4.27 from 332 votes

Course: Dessert

Cuisine: Italian

Keyword: lobster tail pastry, napoli, sfogliatella

Prep Time: 3 hours

Cook Time: 30 minutes

Total Time: 4 hours 30 minutes

Servings: 12 people

Calories: 439kcal

Author: Nonna Box

Chapter 1 Ingredients

Chapter 2 THE DOUGH

- 4 cups flour
- 1 tbsp salt
- 3/4 cup water more if needed
- 3.5 tbsp honey

Chapter 3 THE FILLING

- 1.875 cups whole milk

- 1 cup white sugar
- 1 pinch salt
- 1 cup semolina flour
- 2 cups <u>ricotta</u>
- 1 egg large
- 1/2 teaspoon vanilla extract
- 1 pinch cinnamon
- 2/3 cup candied orange peel finely chopped

Chapter 4 FOR BRUSHING/TOPPING

- 10 tbsp unsalted butter or lard
- Confectioner's sugar

Chapter 5 Instructions

1.   In a large bowl, combine the flour and salt. Add water and honey, and then mix to create a stiff dough. Then gradually add water.

2.   Place the dough on the counter and knead until it's smooth and supple. Wrap in plastic wrap and refrigerate for 30 minutes.

3.   After 30 minutes, split the dough into 4 pieces. Get one piece, then roll through a pasta machine. Roll using the widest setting, then fold in half and roll again. Do the same on each dough. Repeat this process until you create smooth sheets by gradually decreasing the width on each roll.

4.   When the sheet is at 1mm thick, lay it on the surface and apply a thin layer of lard or butter. Create thin sheets of the other doughs as well and roll them into similar thin layers.

5.   Roll up the first thin sheet to create a tight sausage shape.

6.   Next, wrap the next thin dough sheet around the original sausage shape pastry dough, layering up to create one large cylinder. Cover with a saran wrap and chill for 1 to 2 hours for the pastry to firm up.

7.   Now, to make the filling. Place the milk, sugar, and salt in a sauce pan and bring to a boil. Add the semolina flour until it thickens and becomes smooth. After it has cooled down, transfer to a bowl. Then, add the remaining ingredients, stirring all the while to create a smooth, thick filling. Set aside, preferably inside the fridge.

8.   Preheat oven to 375°F.

9.   Bring out the pastry roll and cut them into 1 cm-thick pieces. Use your fingers, greased with lard or butter, to make an impression on the center to create a cone shape.

10.   Get the filling and scoop a spoonful into the hollow and press the edges of the pastry together to lock. Repeat these for the rest, and line up all pastries on the tray.

11.   When you're done putting filling on all the dough pieces, bake the pastries for about 30 minutes.

12.   When done, allow to cool for only a couple of minutes before sprinkling them with confectioner's sugar. Serve immediately.

Chapter 6 Nutrition

Calories: 439kcal | Carbohydrates: 58g | Protein: 12 g | Fat: 18g | Saturated Fat: 11g | Cholesterol: 66mg | Sodium: 158mg | Pot assium: 169mg | Fiber: 2g | Sugar: 16g | Vitamin A: 578IU | Calcium: 142mg | Iron: 3mg

Thank you, dear reader, for buying this book. We admit that we have expensive tastes so your monetary contribution has enabled us to continue to be kept in the style and comfort we deserve. Please tell your friends to buy this book as well, so we may be assured of our continued royal treatment.

Sincerely,

Flossie
Felicity
Flicker
(and in memory of our departed, brother, Freddie.)

The Author's Cats.